Shadow of the Mountain

Shadow of the Mountain

HOLLY AND ROBIN REAMS

CHAPEL HILL
PRESS, INC.

ISBN 978-1-59715-100-9
Library of Congress Catalog Number 2013954526

First Printing

Dedicated to my co-authors:
God and my savior Jesus Christ.
Also in loving memory of my sister.

Holly Reams

1993–2009

I couldn't have written this without constant
help from Heaven. I love you so much!

ROBIN

"The rainbow shall be in the cloud, and I will
look on it to remember the everlasting covenant
between God and every living creature."

GENESIS 9:16

"And now abide faith, hope, love, these three;
but the greatest of these is love."

I CORINTHIANS 13:13

Contents

Acknowledgments..ix

Chapter One...1

Chapter Two...7

Chapter Three..13

Chapter Four..19

Chapter Five...25

Chapter Six...31

Chapter Seven..35

Chapter Eight...43

Chapter Nine..51

Chapter Ten..59

Chapter Eleven...67

Chapter Twelve...75

Chapter Thirteen..83

Chapter Fourteen...91

Chapter Fifteen..99

Chapter Sixteen..107

Chapter Seventeen...117

Chapter Eighteen...125

Chapter Nineteen...135

Chapter Twenty..147

Chapter Twenty-One..155

Chapter Twenty-Two..165

Character Values..175

Get the Scoop...177

Acknowledgments

Again I would like to thank God for igniting my imagination through a group of stray cats in the mountains and giving me the opportunity to publish my first book. I am also very grateful for the expertise and guidance that Edwina Woodbury and Chapel Hill Press, Inc. have given me. Without a doubt I know God put them in my life. Throughout my journey in writing this book, I have been encouraged by so many family and friends. Thank you for your prayers and support. Thanks, Mom and Dad, for helping me fulfill my dream. Finally to Holly, who continues to inspire me.

Chapter One

Warm rays of sunshine streamed through a thicket of blackberry bushes. The unexpected, bright light instantly awoke Shadow from his deep sleep. Turning over he recalled the unusual dream he had. In it something awful was happening to him and his friends. Although he couldn't remember many details, one thing stuck out. He clearly saw some sort of orange things wrapped around the trees in the forest.

Strangely he felt a prickle go down his spine. He tried to tell himself it was only a dream, yet somehow he couldn't shake the feeling something was going to happen. Shuddering in hopes to get rid of the uneasiness, Shadow attempted to get his mind on other thoughts. Easing into a sitting position, he folded his ears down and pushed his arms out into a stretch.

Deciding to take advantage of the warmth, he trotted out of the white-flowered blackberry bush and into the sunshine. Thankfully it was now spring. Life in the forest wasn't all that bad except for the harshly cold winters when fresh kill was scarce. In the past, spring was the most adventurous season. Hunting usually got better, and everything appeared renewed and refreshed.

He looked up at the enormous mountains surrounding the small village in between. The mountains seemed to touch the fluffy, cottonlike clouds slowly drifting in the light blue sky. As the clouds moved, Shadow was amazed at how the Creator formed and directed them through the sky.

Everything the Creator made was awesome, and Shadow often wondered how He made the trees grow and kept the entire world going.

Perhaps I should take advantage of the gorgeous weather and go out for a hunt, Shadow considered.

Giving his black fur coat a few swift licks, he drew a white paw over his left ear. Sudden movements from the blackberry bush made him freeze his swipe in midair. To his relief, the familiar orange-striped coat of Tiger appeared.

Tiger was one of Shadow's friends and a member of the Moonshine Clan. Including Shadow there was a total of five members. They called themselves the Moonshine Clan because they were fascinated by the way the Creator's moon shone so brightly into their blackberry bush home.

"Boy, you sure can tell a difference in the weather. The sunshine feels great!" exclaimed Tiger as he arched his back, showing off his strong muscles.

Always trying to prove he's tough, Shadow observed as he watched Tiger sharpen his claws by biting them. Wonder why he acts like a big shot? His only competition is Midnight.

As if Shadow's private thoughts had summoned him, Midnight came out from the blackberry bush. Sitting down on Shadow's right, the solid black tom let out a delighted purr.

"Good morning, Shadow and Tiger. Spring really might be here for good. The air has a fresh scent, doesn't it?" Midnight remarked.

"But don't forget we aren't out of the water yet. We might be in for a false spring this year," Tiger said with authority.

Glancing from Tiger to Midnight, Shadow was pretty sure neither of them realized he was still there. Tiger had a good point, but there wasn't anything wrong with hoping. Even thunderstorms didn't seem as bad as winter. At least there was fresh food. Surprisingly, Midnight's jet-black fur stayed flat, but the pure fury in his bright yellow eyes couldn't hide his anger.

"Well, Tiger, it never hurt anyone to be cheerful and optimistic," Midnight countered calmly.

Luckily, Cassidy and Destiny came trotting up in time to hear the last comment. Shadow hoped their arrival would keep the peace between the two toms.

"Can't we leave you alone for a few minutes?" implied Destiny with a smile.

"Don't get all worked up, Midnight," Cassidy added, brushing her sandy, striped coat against him lovingly.

Shadow watched as Midnight's expression changed. The love in his eyes showed Cassidy had won him over for now. She could pretty much get him to do anything. How come she-cats always figure out a way to get what they want?

"Why don't we go catch some fresh kill, guys? I'm sure Cassidy and Destiny are hungry," Shadow proclaimed hastily.

"What a wonderful idea, Shadow," replied Cassidy. Then turning to Midnight she added in a loving yet cunning voice, "You and Tiger should go with him. I am rather hungry."

Midnight reluctantly nodded in agreement. Even though he was the wiser of the two, it still took a lot of effort for such a proud cat like Midnight to back down from an equally proud Tiger. Shadow wasn't sure exactly what happened between the toms to make them clash. They had been arguing and competing with each other ever since he first joined the clan. On several different occasions he had mentioned something to Destiny about it, but she evidently didn't know either. Whatever started their rocky relationship must have been bad because neither wanted to give in to the other.

Oddly Midnight had been quieter lately, letting Tiger make his rude comments without fighting back. Shadow knew this had a lot to do with Cassidy. Somehow she had convinced him to stop fussing. The two cats had always been close, but now they were even more bonded—especially since Cassidy was approaching the time to kittening the couple's first litter.

"Are you guys going to stay here daydreaming of mice, or are you going to really catch some?" Tiger questioned.

Without waiting for an answer he trotted off into the center of the forest. Immediately, Midnight followed him with a determined look on his face. Watching the two toms Shadow shook his head.

"Go on, Shadow, try to keep them from fighting," advised Cassidy as she headed toward the blackberry bushes.

"Yeah, and try to bring back some mice and a rabbit," added Destiny.

"I'll do my best," Shadow responded, smiling.

I wonder why Destiny has been a bit on the bossy side lately, Shadow debated with himself. *Never mind, guess I better hustle if I plan on catching up to the toms. Knowing them, they won't wait for me before they start hunting.*

At that, he too set off at a speedy pace in the direction of the woods. He had to practically run to keep up with Midnight and Tiger, who obviously weren't in the mood to hunt together. Finally reaching them, Shadow felt out of breath as the toms split up and went in two directions.

Oh well, determined Shadow, *at least the two of them won't be fighting anymore. Now I can focus on hunting without having to keep the peace.*

Walking briskly through the trees, he decided to go to the edge of the woods where the cornfield was. Last autumn when the leaves were falling, the humans had taken the corn and replaced it with some kind of green, grasslike stuff. Every spring, the humans would come back to turn up the soil from the year before. The huge, noisemaking beasts they used also stirred up the different kinds of bugs and wiggly earthworms, which was what the mice came for. It was a rather complicated matter, but it didn't take Shadow long to figure it out.

By now, the morning sun was well in the sky. As he got closer to the edge of the forest, he slowed down and eased into a crouch. Parting his mouth, Shadow tasted the air for animal scents. At first he didn't taste anything, but then he felt the mouthwatering taste of mouse enter his mouth. Instinctively, Shadow wanted to run out and get him. However, if the game was played right, he might be blessed and catch more than one.

Luckily, the light breeze was blowing away from him, so Shadow's scent didn't drift in its direction. The mouse, which was lazily munching on a reddish-brown earthworm, had no idea Shadow was there. Careful not to step on any dried leaves, Shadow started to slowly crawl toward the brown-furred mouse, making sure his breathing stayed natural.

Just a little bit closer, he judged, almost there.

Within a few feet of the mouse, he stopped. While his belly fur brushed the ground, he lifted his hindquarters and shook them from side to side ready to pounce. For a split second he actually contemplated how he would feel if he were the mouse.

Realizing what he was thinking, he shook his head. How could he possibly think such in the middle of what he was doing? Killing and eating mice and other animals were part of a cat's life. Their survival depended on it even if it did seem cruel. When the Creator made the animals in the world He gave cats the instincts to kill mice and other things for food. Some animals don't eat meat, but cats do, so it is the Creator's will for us to kill for food. After all, even cats were hunted by some creatures.

Refocusing on the task, Shadow checked the distance between him and the mouse once more. Shaking his haunches again, he sprung into the air and onto the mouse. Quickly biting down on its neck, Shadow killed his prey before there was enough time for him to squeak. Acting hastily, he buried the mouse in the ground so a fox wouldn't get his kill.

I'll see if I can kill a rabbit for Destiny. Then I'll come back and get this mouse, Shadow decided. *Midnight will catch something for Cassidy and himself. Tiger, on the other paw, will probably only get enough for one.*

At this thought, Shadow shook his head in distress. Maybe one day, Tiger will think of somebody besides himself all of the time. Turning around, Shadow trotted into a thicket of green-leafed rhododendron bushes to find a rabbit.

Chapter Two

Shadow's heart was pounding against his ribs. His breath was coming heavy and quick as he raced through the maze of maple, pine, and oak trees. As he ran toward the Moonshine Clan's base, he couldn't believe what he had just seen. So much had changed since the other day.

Hopefully Midnight and Tiger are back at the base from hunting, assessed Shadow frantically. *What am I going to do if they aren't? Cassidy's been too tired to leave the base lately with her kits on the way. As for Destiny, with all of the humans in the nearby fields, it's really dangerous to leave Cassidy all alone.*

By now, he was at the blackberry bushes, ducking under the lowest branches. The white flowers were almost gone as they were being replaced by reddish blackberries. In the center was a small clearing where everyone ate their meals. On the far side of the bushes there were thicker branches where the clan slept. As he rushed into the base, Destiny looked up from the gray squirrel she was eating to see what was going on.

"Where are Tiger and Midnight?" Shadow inquired through gasps of breath.

"They're still out hunting. Why?" she answered as Cassidy came out from the sleeping quarters.

"What's going on, Shadow, and why are you breathing so hard?" implied Cassidy, with concern in her hazel eyes.

Still trying to catch his breath, Shadow struggled to answer the she-cats without totally freaking them out. He felt like it was better to tell Tiger and Midnight the serious news first.

"I really need to talk to the guys. It could be something bad or it could be nothing important. I don't want to worry you for no reason," he proclaimed cautiously.

Very aware of the nasty look Destiny gave him, Shadow tried not to take it personally. She did not like it when anyone treated her delicately.

"Come on, you think we're incapable of dealing with important situations?" she questioned while eyeing him.

Striving to choose his words carefully so that she wouldn't get mad, he responded with the best answer he knew.

"No, I just want the guys to be here. I need to at least tell everyone at the same time, don't you think?" he replied.

"Of course, we should wait for Midnight and Tiger," agreed Cassidy.

Looking at her, Destiny appeared completely baffled. Shadow watched the she-cats exchange a quick glance. Destiny's golden yellow eyes showed him she didn't agree with Cassidy at all. Fortunately, Tiger and Midnight came into the center of the blackberry bush before Destiny could object.

Phew, thought Shadow, *they showed up at the perfect moment. Where in the world do I begin? What am I going to do if they don't believe me or think it's not worthy of our concern?* At this thought, Shadow's nerves made his legs wobble with worry. Would his friends take him seriously?

"What happened? Why do you look like you are going to be sick, Shadow?" implied Tiger.

"Yeah, what did we miss? We left you in the woods to hunt, Shadow," Midnight added with confusion.

"Shadow has something important to tell us," explained Cassidy, as she settled down near Midnight.

"He refused to tell us anything until you guys got here," Destiny declared bitterly. Then she added, "Apparently it was so important he didn't even manage to catch any fresh kill."

"Well, Shadow, go ahead and tell us," urged Midnight.

"Okay," he began nervously. "After we split up at the giant maple tree, I went over to the edge of the woods like always. While scenting for any mice or squirrels, the first thing I tasted was the sour scent of humans."

"Shadow," interrupted Tiger, "how birdbrained are you? Didn't you know that the humans come to turn up the dirt every spring?"

Although Tiger said this sarcastically, he was laughing hard and couldn't contain himself. It was obvious he didn't think it was strange for the humans to be so close to the forest. Trying to overlook Tiger's meows of laughter, Shadow picked up where he left off.

"Yes, Tiger, I have scented the faint smell of the humans before, but this time it was a lot stronger. After searching the edge of the woods for any signs of them, I found some kind of orange thing around the biggest trees. Getting closer to have a sniff, this tall human appeared out of nowhere and tied another orange thing to the birch tree beside me. Stopping and realizing I was far enough he couldn't hear me, I slowly eased away. Naturally when it was safe I took off running as fast as my legs would go," he said bluntly.

When he was finished, Shadow looked at his friends, anxious to know what they thought.

Cassidy's hazel eyes were wide with fear, as she crouched close to Midnight. She stared uneasily around the blackberry bush, as if the humans were coming any minute. Tiger's laughter had died away, but he seemed to still be trying to figure out what the humans were doing. Destiny was pushing her unsheathed claws into the black dirt. Her fluffy white fur was standing on ends. As for Midnight, he was staring off in the distance at something unseen. After several moments of complete silence, Midnight spoke up.

"Well, I think we should check this out, but we must be careful. I don't think there is anything to worry about. Let's see what's going on so you won't be worried, Shadow," he proclaimed.

"Yeah, I was about to say the same thing. We'll go have a look to satisfy you, Shadow. Those humans won't have a chance with me, I mean us, around," Tiger added, with a small flicker of embarrassment.

Looking at Midnight, Shadow waited to see if he had heard what Tiger had said, but his expression remained the same. Destiny had obviously heard Tiger's comment, though. She let out an enraged hiss.

"Who do you think you are, Mr. Know-it-all? Think you can handle anything, do you? Go right ahead and fight those humans. Then when you beg for help, we'll see who's really the boss," she shot at him.

Oh boy, Shadow thought, as he prepared himself to separate his friends.

He noticed Midnight and Cassidy were also anxious to see Tiger's reaction. To Shadow's amazement, Tiger just sat there with his orange-striped tail draped neatly across his paws.

"You're right, Destiny. I shouldn't have said what I did. I'm s-s-sorry," he declared, with his head dipped down.

Shadow's jaw dropped in shock. Meanwhile Midnight and Cassidy's eyes grew wide as if they too couldn't believe their ears. Destiny took a step back; she clearly wasn't ready for his apology.

"Oh. Well, you should be," she replied awkwardly.

"We need to go see this orange thing," Midnight advised, leading the way out of the blackberry bush.

"Okay, we'll stay here," announced Destiny, with a sigh as Shadow and Tiger followed Midnight.

Once they were out of the blackberry bush, Midnight stepped aside so Shadow could take the lead. Stepping out in front of his fellow clan mates, Shadow silently hoped the situation wasn't anything too bad.

It wasn't long before the three toms reached the edge of the forest. Slowing down, he tasted the air for the sour scent of the humans. Behind him, Midnight and Tiger did the same. Then, he slowly crept closer to the birch tree where the human was earlier. Although the humans weren't around now, there were twice as many orange things as before.

"What do you think?" inquired Shadow.

"I'm not sure, but hopefully it won't concern us. What's your opinion, Tiger?" Midnight responded.

Tiger didn't answer him because he had walked over to the very edge of the woods. The orange tabby was staring out over the field next to the forest. Midnight and Shadow went to join him.

All of a sudden, Shadow felt a weird sense of danger prickle down his spine. This was the same feeling he had a few days ago after having the strange dream. He recalled those very same orange things being tied to the trees.

Maybe the Creator was giving me a warning about this danger the other day when I had the dream, Shadow considered. *Perhaps the prickle is a sign of what is to come.*

Peering at the field Shadow spotted a new danger. While Shadow had gone to the base, the humans had brought a large number of big beasts into the field. Watching the sun set behind the mountains, Shadow wondered what the humans would do next.

Chapter Three

aindrops poured down from the dark gray clouds hanging low in the sky. Shadow was vigorously licking his damp, mud-caked fur. It had been raining nonstop for the last two days. Unfortunately it didn't seem to be letting up. In fact today seemed to be worse.

Boy, do I hope it will stop soon, he thought. *I can't take much more of this gooey mud. Spring is just getting started, so this is only the beginning.*

After licking his black-furred flank and chest fur, Shadow started cleaning his white paws. He knew the Creator supplied rain for a reason, but it still frustrated him.

You can't even tell my paws are white, they look browner to me, he reflected with annoyance. *What good is it going to do me to keep my fur clean? All I'm going to do is go right back into the woods and hunt. Can't you give me a break, Mighty Creator?*

With this concept, Shadow let out an agitated sigh of disgust. He actually loathed the rainy season because of the endless cycle of having to lick himself clean over and over again. Out of the corner of his eye, he spotted Tiger trotting toward him from the sleeping quarters.

"Clean yet?" Tiger asked, his whiskers twitching in amusement.

"For now," Shadow responded, grinning. "Let me guess, you want me to go hunting with you and get all muddy again."

"Yep, you guessed right," answered Tiger. "I suppose that means you will go with me then?"

"Sure, what's a hundred more licks! I've already coughed up a few hair balls. I think I need some green grass. Did Midnight say if he was coming?" Shadow inquired.

"He said he would catch up with us later on this afternoon. The hard rain last night somehow broke through parts of our sleeping quarters. He wants to fix it so Cassidy won't catch a cold since she was sneezing," Tiger admitted.

"Okay, well, I'm ready when you are. Lead the way," Shadow proclaimed, as he motioned with his tail for Tiger to go first.

Reluctantly, Shadow followed Tiger by brushing his chest fur against the muddy ground to go under the low-hanging blackberry branches. Once the two of them were out in the open, the friends bounded off toward the giant maple tree in the center of the forest.

By now, it was raining so hard Shadow could barely see where they were going. With their pelts plastered to their bodies and ears folded back, the toms zigzagged through the maze of trees. Their paws matched each other step for step, despite the horrible conditions.

When the two toms reached the massive, knobby roots of the giant maple tree, they slowed up. They made their way across the roots to sit beside the trunk. It made a perfect shelter from the rain.

As the tomcats sat side by side, they gazed in the direction of the corn-field. The landscape spread out before them was a horrifying one. Both of them had of course seen the destruction many times over the past three or four days, but it was still mind-boggling.

Shadow had been right. The humans were up to something. For the last several days since his discovery, the humans had used their beasts to destroy the forest. Only the few birch, maple, and ash trees with orange things on them remained. Other trees lay in piles all over the forest floor. As for the orange flame azaleas, pink redbuds, and other undergrowth, they too had been crushed. Rabbits, squirrels, and birds had retreated farther into the woods, but they were now harder to get to.

Clearly, the Moonshine Clan was definitely going to have a tough spring, not to mention the summer. With so much destruction, Shadow wondered if the animals in the forest could survive. After all, their survival depended heavily on the abundance of fresh meat.

"It doesn't even seem natural," Tiger whispered in a hoarse tone.

"No, it doesn't. I just hope the humans don't come any closer. We can't live in a place with no food or shelter. There's no way we can fight them when we're getting weaker, you know," Shadow commented.

"We are not going to back down!" exclaimed Tiger furiously. Sitting back down he continued more calmly, "I'm sorry, Shadow. I know you are only telling the truth. It's just hard for me to think about us not being able to stop those humans. What did we ever do to them to deserve this punishment?"

"I don't know, Tiger," Shadow replied. He paused before adding, "Let's go catch some fresh kill."

Tiger grimly nodded and sprinted through the downpour over to some green-leafed rhododendrons. There were a few that hadn't been touched by the beasts yet. Shadow watched the orange-striped pelt of his friend disappear into the bushes. Then he turned his attention back to the devastated forest.

He let his gaze sweep over the wrecked debris before darting toward the budding rhododendrons. To his dismay, Shadow again felt the same, uneasy feeling of trouble prickle down his spine. For some reason he had been having the same tingle repeatedly over the last two days. Clearly the Creator was trying to tell him something, but what?

Letting his thoughts control him, Shadow recollected the past few days. *Why does the Creator keep giving me these strange feelings? Does it mean our problems aren't over? Will our predicament actually get worse? It's like I already know something bad is going to happen.*

Shadow tried to put his crazy ideas aside and hunt, but he just couldn't concentrate. The rain didn't help things. In fact it seemed to be getting harder and the graying sky had almost turned black by now. Parting his jaws Shadow tasted the air, but no matter how he tried, no scents came to him.

Finally, he decided to withdraw from hunting and find Tiger. Scenting the damp air yet again, Shadow searched for Tiger's smell. He reminded himself that Tiger's scent was probably slightly muffled because of the immense amount of precipitation. Following a small trace of Tiger's scent around some pink redbud flowers, Shadow found him digging up a mouse he had buried. Apparently Tiger had picked up on his own scent.

"Hey, Shadow, I was just coming to find you. Did you manage to catch anything?" he inquired.

"No, I didn't; looks like you did, though. By the way, have you seen Midnight?" Shadow questioned.

"Nope, let's go back to the base and see what is keeping him," Tiger responded, as he picked up his mouse and trotted off toward the blackberry bush.

Nodding in agreement, Shadow trotted after the orange tabby. When the toms reached the bush, they scrambled under the limbs. Glad to be somewhat sheltered from the downpour, Shadow let out a purr of pleasure. Then he and Tiger bounded across the small clearing to the sleeping quarters. No sooner had Tiger dropped his mouse, Destiny unexpectedly appeared from within the thick branches.

"Where have you been?" she demanded.

"Out hunting, why? Where is Midnight? We were waiting for him to join us, but he never showed up," Shadow questioned her.

"He's with Cassidy in the sleeping quarters. While the two of you were hunting this morning she had her kittens!" Destiny announced, with her golden yellow eyes gleaming in excitement.

"Wow!" Shadow declared in astonishment.

"How many kittens do Cassidy and Midnight have?" Tiger asked in a surprisingly interested tone.

"She had three healthy kittens, two little girls and a tiny boy. They have already named them and everything," Destiny proclaimed in a thrilled voice.

"How's Cassidy doing? Is she resting? Can we see the kittens?" Shadow questioned enthusiastically.

"She's tired but I'm sure she won't mind showing off her sweet little babies. Come on, follow me," she answered.

Bouncing with happiness, Destiny led Shadow and Tiger into the thick branches of the sleeping quarters. Shadow was so thrilled to meet the new arrivals he could hardly restrain himself from shouting with joy. He had really been looking forward to seeing these kittens.

The three of them made their way to the back of the thickest part of the blackberry bush where Midnight and Cassidy were. Cassidy was resting on her right side on some soft green moss. Midnight was lying next to her, his yellow eyes overflowing with pride and happiness. When they drew closer, both Cassidy and Midnight raised their heads with proud smiles.

"Hey, guys! Sorry I didn't make it out hunting, when this situation unfolded my mind slipped. I'm still in shock actually and had no idea I was going to become a dad today," Midnight told them.

"It's really too messy to hunt anyway. The rain has pretty much washed away most of the scents. We brought you the mouse we caught. That's all we could manage," Tiger responded, as he pushed the mouse in their direction.

Picking up the soggy mouse, Tiger dropped it at Midnight's paws. Still seated beside Cassidy, Midnight quickly tore the meat in bite-sized pieces so that she could easily eat while the kits nursed.

"We really appreciate the mouse, Tiger, but I think you found this one swimming in the creek. He's soaking wet!" Midnight teased.

"Ha, ha, very funny," Tiger replied as he shook his head.

Destiny, Cassidy, and Shadow laughed at Midnight's joke. Despite the fact Tiger tried hard to hide it, he too was chuckling.

"Yes, thank you both," Cassidy proclaimed. "I'm sure you are all eager to meet the newest members of the clan. Right now they are blind and deaf, but in about ten days their eyes and ears should open up. We named this kitten Lily."

Cassidy flicked her tail tip at one of the three kits. This one was a solid black kitten. Using her muzzle, she carefully touched the second kit, a sand-colored kitten with a white-colored underbody.

"This one's name is Daisy," she said. Then nodding toward the tiny, sand-colored kitten on the end she added, "And the tom's name is Milo."

"They are so precious and adorable!" exclaimed Destiny. "I'm glad everything turned out okay. This was a miraculous event and a wonderful blessing from the Creator!"

"You are absolutely right, Destiny. The Creator has blessed us greatly!" Cassidy agreed with a tired smile.

"It's amazing how small and helpless they are. I can already tell they will make life exciting! Congratulations!" Shadow added, grinning.

While Midnight asked Tiger about the human activity, Destiny gave Cassidy some of the poppy flower seeds and spiky, purple-flowered catnip they had collected a moon ago. They kept poppy seeds for pain and catnip for colds or fevers as well as spiderwebs to stop bleeding.

Listening to his friends talk, Shadow's mind wandered back to the kittens. Secretly, he could barely hold back his excitement. He couldn't wait until the newest members of the clan were old enough to play with. For some reason he felt especially attached to the tiny tom, Milo. These kittens were the greatest!

Chapter Four

usts of cold wind hailed Shadow. He wasn't accustomed to the chilly mountain air that usually greeted him this time of year. Today looked like it would be particularly windy. The mountains surrounding the forest had been sending down the harsh, cold winds all morning. Shadow regretted offering to get food for the Moonshine Clan.

Why in the world does it have to be so cold this morning? he pondered. *It's supposed to be getting warmer. I can't go back to the base without something to eat, though. Tiger and Midnight would be furious if I broke my promise. They are counting on me to do my part.*

Trotting over to some purple-flowered rhododendrons, Shadow made his way to the giant maple tree in the center of the forest. Opening his mouth, he scented the air for anything edible. The smell coming to his nose was definitely not a mouse, but it was an animal. As he tried to figure out what kind of animal the scent belonged to, a voice sounded behind Shadow scaring the living daylights out of him.

"Boo!" exclaimed a cheerful voice.

Shadow whipped around to see who had spoken. Acting on instinct his black fur stood straight out, making Shadow's body seem twice as big. This was something every cat did to fend off enemies by appearing much more powerful than they were.

"Don't be such a scaredy-cat!" laughed Destiny, as she flicked him with her fluffy white tail.

With relief flooding over him, Shadow realized the scent was hers. Relaxing a bit, his fur coat slowly laid back down while he attempted to calm his pounding heart. He secretly felt ashamed he had been scared so easily.

"Oh, it's you. Why did you scare me so bad?" he questioned her, trying not to show how frightened he had really been.

"Sorry, I didn't mean to scare you. I just wanted to have a little fun. Have you caught anything yet?" Destiny implied.

Shadow couldn't help but smile at his friend. She had really changed since the birth of Cassidy's kittens and her attitude had become pleasantly joyful.

Grinning, Shadow answered, "Not so far, but I really haven't had much of a chance. I went to observe the humans first. They were bringing some kind of long pieces of wood into the clearing. I was in the process of hunting for something when you snuck up on me."

"Do you mind going with me to see what the humans are doing? I haven't seen the wreckage in a while," she told him.

"Okay," he agreed, "but we should hunt first. You know what Tiger will say if we show up with nothing."

"Oh, yes!" she blurted out.

Destiny puffed out her white chest fur and strutted around Shadow trying to mimic Tiger. Although he didn't think it was right to make fun of Tiger, it was still hilarious.

"Well, well, well, what do we have here? It seems like somebody didn't do their part for the clan. I would not have done such a thing. I would have caught something to eat or not come back until I did. Don't ever do it again," she imitated in a bossy, sarcastic way.

She and Shadow burst out in laughter at her entertaining performance, though she did admit she shouldn't have done so. They both knew how important Tiger thought he was. After getting themselves under control, the two friends trotted over to a group of birch trees hoping to find food.

Shadow stopped to scent the air with his muzzle. Concentrating hard, he instantly recognized the smell of some kind of bird nearby.

Destiny had obviously scented the bird, too. She was staring in the direction of some pinkish-white, star-shaped mountain laurels. As she did so, she eased herself into a hunter's crouch.

Following her gaze to the mountain laurel bushes, Shadow saw it was a brownish-black, ruffed grouse pecking the ground around the bushes in search of insects. The striped, black feathers along its back proved it was a male. Shadow figured the grouse had ventured to this part of the forest while looking for a female to start a family.

He noticed the grouse wore a ring of ruffed feathers around its neck. This reminded him of seeing the chickenlike bird in the snow last winter. Unlike most of the other birds, the grouse wouldn't fly south for the harsh winters. Instead, they grew bristled leg feathers to keep their feet warm.

Another thing that bewildered Shadow was the way the Creator formed weblike stuff between their toes. The grouse would grow this every year before the snow season. It enabled them to actually walk on top of the deep snowdrifts.

Shadow knew these birds were not only fast but also very smart. He had tried numerous times to catch one with no luck at all. Strangely they always found a way to escape his grasps. Hopefully with Destiny's helpful assistance the two of them could capture the creature this time. After all, the feathered bird was large enough to feed the entire Moonshine Clan.

While he had been watching the grouse, Destiny had cleverly crept and positioned herself within several feet of him. She raised her haunches and shook them from side to side, preparing to jump on the bird. Then without making a sound, she expertly leaped into the air in the bird's direction. Despite her careful execution of a skilled hunter's attack, the grouse saw her coming and set off through the woods at a pace no cat could follow.

"Rats!" Destiny hissed out of frustration and disappointment. "We almost had the grouse in our claws."

"It's okay we'll find something else to eat. Don't worry, Destiny," Shadow assured her. "Besides, I don't like all the feathers anyway, do—," he added as he was interrupted.

Shadow hesitated when a rustling sound came from some nearby purple rhododendrons. Instantly, he and Destiny glanced at each other, mutually agreeing to be still. Smelling the air, Shadow was able to decipher what kind of creature was hiding inside the bush. The animal was definitely a squirrel. Destiny, who had evidently scented the air herself, signaled with a twitch of her whiskers for him to go in for the kill. Knowing he would have to work fast, Shadow crouched down so his black belly fur brushed the ground.

At that moment, the squirrel appeared. It had grayish-brown fur and the fluffiest tail you could imagine. The squirrel was holding a partially eaten acorn in its small paws. His back was turned toward Shadow, enabling him the chance to creep closer to his target. Amazingly the squirrel was working on his acorn fast. Shadow's eyes couldn't keep up with its swiftly moving paws.

When Shadow was within killing distance, the squirrel turned around to find another acorn. Surprised to see an attacker, he whipped back around to dash off to a nearby maple tree. Luckily, Destiny had his escape route blocked. Seeing there was no way out, the squirrel started chattering angrily and flipping his puffed-out tail in all directions.

Unsheathing his claws, Shadow let them sink into the ground before raising his hindquarters and shaking them from side to side. Pouncing onto the squealing gray squirrel, he quickly sank his teeth into its soft, furry neck. The defeated squirrel let out one last, shrill cry before going limp in Shadow's jaws. Feeling very pleased, Shadow purred with happiness.

"Thank you for helping me corner the squirrel, Destiny. I couldn't have done it without your assistance," he announced.

"No problem! Maybe Tiger won't be mad now. Can we go see the humans?" she pleaded eagerly.

Nodding his approval, Shadow picked up the squirrel and followed her to the giant maple tree. Once they were at the tree, he dropped the squirrel meat and settled down next to Destiny. The humans were busy using the wood Shadow had seen earlier. They were building some sort of shelters.

"Do you suppose the humans will live in those things they are making?" Destiny asked with curiosity.

"I have no idea. I don't know what else they could use them for, though. What doesn't make sense is why they are building so many of them. Surely the small amount of humans can't possibly fill all those places," he replied.

Destiny nodded and advised him, "We better head home."

Both of them made their way to the blackberry bush. When they entered the base, Shadow saw Cassidy and the three kittens right away. She had her kits near the entrance of the sleeping quarters.

The kits' eyes were now open as they began to wiggle around some. Shadow loved watching them as they struggled to learn how to walk. They kept falling over while attempting to walk with their teeny-tiny claws. Right now Daisy, the sand-and-white-colored kitten, was curled up next to her mother. Lily was lying next to her sister, but her solid black fur made her almost invisible against the ground.

As Shadow watched, he realized one kitten wasn't there. For a split second he panicked as he wondered what happened to the third kit. Then he spotted the sand-colored tom, Milo, outside. At this moment Destiny, who had also been watching, went over to Milo and picked him up by his scruff of his neck. Squealing with protest, little Milo squirmed in her jaws.

"Thank you, Destiny," Cassidy declared when she brought back her son. "He's already wandering off and getting into trouble," she added with a smile.

Shadow dropped the squirrel down next to Cassidy.

"This is for you, Cassidy," he told her. "You should eat so you will stay strong and healthy for the kittens."

"Is that all you caught?" exclaimed Tiger's bossy voice.

Turning around, Shadow spotted Tiger and Midnight trotting toward them. The two toms had apparently been out hunting as well, though neither of them carried any fresh kill.

"Yes, do you have a problem? At least we managed to bring back something. It doesn't look like you killed anything," demanded Destiny angrily.

Tiger opened his mouth to shoot something back, but Midnight cut him off.

"Stop fighting, you two. The four of us will eat what Cassidy doesn't. We all know the food is getting scarce, and we should be thankful for anything the Creator provides us with," he stated calmly.

Shadow knew Midnight was right. One squirrel wasn't nearly enough for the five of them to survive on for very long. He wondered what would happen if the food and shelter went away completely.

Deep down Shadow was aware of the fact that he and his friends wouldn't live long. He looked toward Midnight and Tiger. They were both too proud to admit the clan couldn't make it. Gazing at Destiny and Cassidy, he knew they were scared to death of the humans. Shadow finally set his eyes on the three kits. Even with their mother's milk, their tiny ribs were already showing. How much longer could they survive?

Chapter Five

Mouthwatering tastes of fresh kill entered Shadow's parted jaws. He was standing in the center of the forest at the old maple tree. All around him were strong trances of rabbit, mouse, and squirrel scents. The mixture of scents made his head swim in circles. Part of him wanted to hunt down something to eat, but the other part just wanted to sit and enjoy the aroma.

As he sat there trying to decide which to do, Shadow let his gaze sweep over the forest. All sorts of hardwoods, low-lying shrubs, and wildflowers were everywhere. The Creator had made the forest a perfect haven for all of the animals that depended on it.

While Shadow was studying the forest, an unexpected thought struck him at the same time. What happened to the multitudes of human shelters? Strangely the wooded forest appeared to be completely untouched by them.

All of a sudden, a booming noise echoed through Shadow's mind. Jerking, the noise brought him back into the real world. Startled by what had just happened, he realized he must have been dreaming.

Since he was awake he recalled having heard the booming sound before. Every year during the springtime mating season, the male grouse would make this sound to attract females. They would find a fallen log and sit on it. Then they would make the earsplitting, booming noise. At first, Shadow thought the grouse was hitting the log with its wings. After watching its blurred wings several times, he found out it was just an illusion.

It's probably the same male grouse Destiny and I attempted to capture the other day, determined Shadow to himself.

Thinking about the hunt, Shadow was reminded of the forest and the human activity nearby. He bitterly realized the dream he had just woken up from was too good to be true.

By now the forest was completely ruined. Only a few trees and bushes remained around their blackberry bush camp. Humans had put up so many shelters, Shadow couldn't count them all.

Reviewing his dream, Shadow could almost taste the animals' scents. An intense pang of hunger engulfed him at the thought of fresh food. The Moonshine Clan hadn't caught anything except one mouse in the past two days. Of course, the mouse, which looked undernourished itself, had been given to Cassidy, who was still nursing the kittens.

Shadow knew he needed to go look for food again, but he could hardly stand up. Pushing himself into a sitting position, he unsheathed his claws into a stretch. He then swept his dark green eyes over his friends sleeping all around him.

Midnight and Cassidy were sleeping close together with their three kits. Tiger was near the entrance, the farthest from everyone else because of his tendency to snore a lot. Destiny, on the other paw, slept next to where Shadow was sitting.

As he sat there watching his friends sleep, Shadow mulled over why she had suddenly wanted to be with him lately. During the past days they had spent a lot of time hunting and talking. Their relationship seemed to grow as brother and sister. In fact she even shared with him her feelings about what it might be like to have a family like Cassidy.

Getting up, Shadow quietly made his way around Tiger and out of the sleeping quarters. Once he was outside, he started to give his black fur coat a good licking. He noticed his bony ribs were almost visible beneath his coat, despite his black fur. It had been a whole moon since the humans had come to the forest.

We can't continue to stay here, Shadow calculated. *If we do the humans will kill us by completely taking our food and water supply away. Where will we be by the next moon? When the moon is full again, there won't be anything left of the forest or our clan. Why can't the Creator protect us? Isn't He powerful enough to stop the humans?*

This left Shadow's heart in a turmoil. He was angry, unhappy, confused, and scared. What were they going to do?

"Haven't you licked yourself enough yet?" asked a voice from behind.

Shadow turned his head just in time to see Destiny's fluffy white body coming toward him.

"I suppose so," he replied. "What are the others doing?"

"Well," proclaimed Destiny, "Midnight is trying to help Cassidy bring the kittens outside for some fresh air."

"How about Tiger?" Shadow questioned.

"Tiger went hunting. Didn't you see him leave?" she answered in confusion.

"No, I guess I wasn't paying attention," he muttered.

Just then, Midnight interrupted their conversation by placing one of the kittens on the ground between them. Upon closer examination, Shadow realized it was Lily, the solid black kit.

"Watch her for me," the black tom declared, as he went back to help Cassidy with the other two.

It wasn't long before he returned with Daisy, the sand-and-white-colored kit. This time, Cassidy followed him carrying the sand-colored tom, Milo. She carefully gathered her precious kittens closer to her. Once they were settled, the four adult cats began to talk about how much the kittens had grown. Amazingly they were now a half a moon old. As they were talking, Tiger came bursting into the clearing breathing hard. Behind him lay a trail of blood.

"Tiger, you're bleeding!" exclaimed Destiny, moving toward him as he collapsed to the ground in exhaustion.

"What happened?" asked Shadow, going over to his friend's aid.

"I was hunting near the giant maple tree, when one of those beasts came toward me. It knocked down a tree, which gave me this," he responded, as he nodded at the deep gash along his side.

While he spoke, Destiny ran into the sleeping quarters. Returning, she pressed green moss on Tiger's wound and covered it with spiderwebs to stop the bleeding, making him wince in pain. Shadow noticed she had unopened poppy seeds with her.

"What are we going to do? We can't continue to live like this. How can we? We don't have any food or shelter, and now one of us has gotten injured," Midnight proclaimed.

"I know what I'm going to do!" announced Tiger, as he strained to sit up.

"You are not going to do anything until your side stops bleeding," indicated Destiny. "Here, eat these poppy seeds. They will help with the pain."

She gave him a nasty look, as if to say he had no choice but to obey her until his side had stopped bleeding. Reluctantly, the orange tabby ate the seeds.

"Well, when the bleeding does stop, I will fight those humans with everything I've got," he stated furiously.

"You can't be serious! They will only kill us. No, we can't stay here and fight a battle no cat can win. Maybe we could become a human's pet," Midnight recommended.

"What? How birdbrained are you?" demanded Tiger. "I am not going to allow those humans to turn me into some prissy kitty cat. I would rather die with dignity. You are not the boss of me! If you want to live like that, fine. Take Cassidy and the kits and go. Meanwhile, I will prove to everyone what a true cat does," Tiger countered angrily.

Unfortunately, Shadow knew their dilemma had now opened up a new issue: who was the leader of the clan. In his personal opinion, it wasn't really an important problem, although Tiger and Midnight obviously thought it was. Shadow also knew neither of them would give in to the other, which was what scared him the most. The clan definitely did not need to be fighting right now. There were more critical problems going on.

"You aren't my boss either," replied Midnight, who was equally enraged. "If you want to die, go right ahead. Unlike you, I have to think of somebody besides myself. We can't live here anymore and you know it. I'm not staying here to watch my family starve to death," he related back.

This time Cassidy spoke up, "Please, Midnight, don't argue! We shouldn't be fighting among ourselves. I'm not sure what decision needs to be made, but fighting will not help."

"Cassidy is absolutely right. Fighting is not the answer. We must stick together," Destiny agreed, as she allowed Tiger to sit up. Then she added, "As far as who is in command, I don't remember appointing anyone."

Shadow, who had up until now been silent, decided he needed to say what was on his heart. Taking a nervous breath, he began.

"Guys, I want to say something. For one thing, we should stay together and stop fussing. None of us is the leader. There is no reason why we can't do this as a clan. Midnight, I understand your thoughts, but the humans won't keep us all together. Tiger, you are a brave cat, but you are foolish to think we can stop the humans. If nothing else, we have learned the humans are dangerous. There's no stopping them, until they get their way. Girls, you also have an opinion on this; however, I think my idea might be the most reasonable."

"So you have a solution, do you? Well, let's hear what your genius idea is," Tiger snapped.

Shadow could tell he wasn't happy. Tiger always thought his ideas were better than anyone else's. Despite Tiger's sour attitude, Shadow didn't let it bother him. Everyone knew Cassidy and Destiny usually agreed with him in the end.

"In my opinion, we should leave the forest for good. Perhaps we can go to the village and live there. I don't want to leave any more than you do, but we don't have an alternative. It would be hard; however, it's better than being a kitty cat or dead. This way we'll stay together, and we can raise the kits as proper forest cats," Shadow advised his friends.

"Your idea does make sense, Shadow. I can't think of any other way, so I guess Cassidy and I will go with you," muttered Midnight solemnly.

"It doesn't look like I have a choice in the matter," Tiger remarked.

"No, you don't! We are a clan and the decision we make together is the one we all must go along with. Your vote is outnumbered four to one," Destiny exclaimed.

"Destiny has a point. At least we'll all stay together," Cassidy declared.

Chapter Six

Thrusting himself underneath the blackberry bush Shadow entered into the small clearing. The ground was still damp from last night's rain. Although the crisp winds blowing down from the mountaintops were steadily drying it out, the ground still was a muddy mess.

Early this morning, Shadow was lucky enough to catch a squirrel. Since returning, he trotted over to the sleeping quarters. He was delighted to find the squirrel, and to have not been caught in the downpour.

The smell of his fresh kill right under his nose made him wild with hunger. Shadow knew he had to share with the other members of the Moonshine Clan. Everyone needed the meat for extra strength. Today was the day the clan would begin their journey to the village. Shadow was excited to be exploring a new place, but the aspect of leaving his beloved woodland home tore him apart. He and his friends had no other choice, if they wanted to survive.

Wonder why the humans did this to us, he debated angrily. *Surely they know the Creator made us animals, too. It doesn't seem right to just come and take our home by destroying the forest little by little. Then again, nothing seems to be fair lately.*

Coming to a stop in front of the sleeping quarters, Shadow dropped his kill. Peering inside he called out to his friends.

"Is anyone up yet? I killed a fresh squirrel for all of us to share," he announced into the dark tunnel.

After a few minutes of silence, the fluffy white body of Destiny emerged. Yawning, she greeted Shadow with a smile.

"Good morning! Did I hear you say something about food?" she implied sleepily as her stomach growled with hunger.

"Yes, you did," he answered, smiling in return.

Behind Destiny, Tiger's orange-striped pelt appeared. The tabby tom stretched his muscles, revealing his bony ribs, and winced in pain from his injury.

"Morning, Shadow. Boy, am I still sore," he declared. Sitting down next to Shadow, he added to Destiny, "Sleep well?"

"Somewhat," she responded.

Before Destiny had a chance to continue, Midnight walked out of the sleeping quarters. Despite the fact that he wore a worried look on his face, the black tom attempted to sound cheerful and energized.

"Good morning, all! If you don't mind I'll take our portion to Cassidy," he announced.

"Okay, Midnight, sounds good," agreed Shadow.

Midnight picked up the squirrel in his jaws and tore off enough for the two of them. With a nod he trotted back to Cassidy carrying their part of the squirrel. After watching him go, Shadow bent down to tear the remaining meat into three pieces. Thanking the Creator, he ate his portion quickly, grateful to have anything at all. Although the meat didn't fill him up, it still gave him some energy. Once he finished eating, he looked up to see Tiger and Destiny had also devoured their portions.

"I'll go get Midnight and Cassidy. I'm sure they need help with the kittens. We should probably get a head start on the journey to the village," Destiny muttered in a small voice.

She disappeared into the sleeping quarters. When she returned she was carrying Milo. Behind her came Cassidy with Lily, and Midnight carrying Daisy. The three of them set the kittens down and looked at Shadow, as if waiting for a command. Shadow was startled by this; nobody ever listened to him. He was even more baffled when he noticed Tiger staring.

"I'm not your leader, guys. We are in this together and should make our decisions as a clan," he muttered.

"We know, but you figured out what we needed to do," Destiny answered.

Shadow noticed the she-cats seemed to be the ones wanting him to lead. The toms, on the other paw, looked down at their paws as if they didn't agree with them. His friends had obviously discussed the issue while he was out getting food this morning.

"It doesn't matter who figured it out; however, I do think we need to ask the Creator for guidance before we begin the journey," Shadow advised.

Everyone nodded in agreement and closed their eyes to honor the Creator.

"Mighty Creator," Midnight began. "Thank You for all You do for us. Protect us on this journey and please provide us with food and shelter. May Your will be done."

"Alright, is everyone ready to go?" Destiny inquired.

"I think we are now. Cassidy and I have decided I will carry Lily," announced Midnight. Then he added, "Cassidy wanted Daisy to go with you, Destiny. And Milo can go with—."

"I can take Milo," Shadow volunteered as Midnight nodded his approval.

"Fine with me. I would rather watch out for humans, to be honest. My side is still sore," declared Tiger, jumping up to go.

"Since you are taking the kits, I'll be by your sides to reassure them they are safe," Cassidy said, as she looked at her three tiny kittens.

"Let's go," muttered Tiger, glancing around the clearing.

Without another look, the orange tabby trotted out of the blackberry bush. Midnight and Cassidy quickly followed him, carrying Lily in his mouth. Destiny looked at her forest home once more.

"Come on, Shadow, it's time for us to leave," she reminded him as she picked Daisy up and made her way out of the camp.

Shadow let his gaze sweep over his beloved home. Sadly this would be the very last time he would ever see it. Trying to catch up with the others, he carefully picked up Milo by the scruff of his tiny neck. Shadow headed toward the lowest branches of the blackberry bush. He looked over his shoulder once more as he pushed himself out into the open.

The humans' incredible destruction was now up to the clan's main territory. As Shadow glanced over the totally devastated forest, a sharp pang of sorrow and distress pulsed through his heart. Deep down he knew he would never be able to do anything else in these woods again. He couldn't take anything with him except the fond memories in his heart.

Slowly trotting off, the Moonshine Clan headed in the direction of the village. After walking through a pasture of tall green grass, they climbed one by one up a small grass-covered hill, as far as any of them had ever ventured. From now on, the clan would be traveling through unknown territory.

Once the group had made it to the top of the ridge, they turned back to catch a glimpse of the forest they adored so much. Now that the downpour of rain had stopped, a beautifully colored rainbow stretched high above them. The brilliant red, orange, yellow, green, blue, and purple arches extended far beyond the highest mountaintops. This awesome scene showed that the Creator had an elaborate imagination.

Shadow was glad the storm clouds had cleared up for the time being. He knew the gorgeous rainbow meant the rain would not start back for a while. Hopefully without a downpour, the clan could cover a considerable amount of distance. As Shadow looked up at the rainbow, a thought struck him.

After every rainstorm, there is a beautiful rainbow. Wonder if the same thing goes for our situation. If our problems are similar to thunderstorms, then some kind of rainbow will follow them. Maybe something good will happen from the horrible pain we have been put through.

While staring into the clouds at the rainbow, Shadow felt a little bit better. He had never thought about the rainbow being a promise from the Creator. Inside his heart, a tiny flicker of hope sparked to life. Perhaps this small desire for a better life will come true. Sometimes, wishes do happen to those who believe the hardest. With renewed faith, Shadow and his friends continued toward the village.

Chapter Seven

aybreak was just minutes away, as the starry night's sky was steadily growing lighter. Now awake, Shadow watched the slowly fading stars with interest—a magnificent sight that anyone would have been lucky to glimpse. Normally, the branches on the blackberry bush would block out this marvelous scene. Out here in the open fields, there wasn't anything to obscure it. The waiting process was long, yet Shadow felt it was well worth it.

The pinkish-orange rays of sunlight emerged from behind the surrounding mountaintops in the horizon. Shadow smiled gracefully at the sight of the miraculous scene of nature. He never realized how breathtaking daybreak was to watch and never took the time to see the Creator's simple yet powerful design.

Behind him, his friends were just waking up. The kittens were now too big to carry, which meant the trip was taking longer than they had originally anticipated. Even though they weren't quite weaned, they were starting to get into everything possible. Shadow had no idea kittens were so curious and rambunctious. Milo seemed to be the worst of the three. He was always either running off or constantly bombarding Shadow with hundreds of questions.

Just then, Milo came up to him.

"Hello, Shadow! Dad said we needed to get started on the last part of our journey to the village," the youngster proclaimed, bouncing in excitement.

"We are going to be able to finish the trip today, right, Shadow?" he added with less confidence.

"Hopefully, Milo," Shadow replied grinning.

"We better get moving, if we plan to get to the village before the sun sets tonight. I know it's rather early in the morning, but there is a whole lot of ground to cover," announced Tiger.

While Shadow had been discussing travel plans with young Milo, the other members of the Moonshine Clan were getting ready to leave. In Shadow's opinion, the most dangerous events of the expedition were yet to come. The remaining part of the journey involved more humans.

Tiger started trotting toward the village. Midnight ran to catch up with Tiger so he wouldn't get too far ahead. They were both assuming their usual leadership duties, which got annoying at times. Cassidy and Destiny followed the toms, trotting so close together their pelts brushed. Beside them, Lily and Daisy tried to copy the older she-cats.

Milo looked up at Shadow, as if asking permission to walk with him. Shadow gave him a nod of approval. Then he fell in line with the others, keeping a sharp eye on Milo. He had to admit Milo had a lot of spunk and energy—maybe a little too much enthusiasm.

Shadow watched the small kitten move a little ahead. His long, sand-colored tail was swaying from side to side. Realizing he was mimicking Destiny, his sisters, and his mother, Shadow couldn't help but chuckle in amusement. Milo then turned to see if he was watching. Next, he pushed out his chest fur like Tiger and his father. Again he looked to see if Shadow was watching. By now, Shadow could hardly contain himself, as he observed Milo strutting in front.

It was obvious Milo was rather fond of him. He understood, because he was aware of the fact that young Milo didn't get as much attention from his parents as his two sisters did. Checking to see if anyone else was looking, Shadow puffed out his chest fur and started to prance along with Milo.

Before long the Moonshine Clan came to the outskirts of the busy village. The village looked like a wondrous place full of adventure and, of course, more humans. There were shelters for them to live in and some sort of black rock paths for them all over the place.

Soon the group of cats came up to one of the black rock paths. Shadow realized that in order to make it to the village, the clan would have to cross it. The humans apparently traveled through the maze of rock paths on their beasts.

As the clan approached the path, Shadow tasted the air for any humans or other dangers. Instantly, a vile taste entered his parted jaws. It was such a strong sensation, he felt a bit queasy. He figured the scent must be coming from the rock paths.

The clan stopped within a few paw steps of the rock path. Shadow noticed his friends all wore grim faces—not only from the reeking odor, but also from the peril they were about to encounter.

They watched as a beast hurried past as it headed north toward the village. It wasn't as big as the ones in the field back home, and the circle things were different. Zooming by, it blasted the cats with an intense wind, almost knocking them off their paws. When it was out of sight, Tiger bravely stood up and faced his fellow clan mates.

"I'll go first. We must be careful, though, and make sure you look out for any beasts before crossing," he declared.

"Wait a second, Tiger," Midnight advised. "Your shoulder hasn't completely healed. You might have trouble crossing alone. Plus, we don't know what's on the other side. I'll go instead."

Tiger shook his head as he replied, "No, no, no, you have to help your family across, Midnight."

Shadow interrupted at this point.

"Let me go, guys. I'm healthier, for one reason, and I don't have any kits," he suggested.

Midnight and Tiger looked at each other for a moment before nodding solemnly in agreement. Stepping back, the two of them moved out of the way so Shadow could approach the edge of the black rock path. Moving forward he was able to see clearly in both directions.

Secretly, Shadow was scared to death, but he would never admit his true feelings. He had to make this sacrifice for his clan. Between the path's reeking smell and his nerves, Shadow felt sure he was going to be sick.

Looking at his friends one last time, Shadow took a deep breath and looked both ways. Everything seemed to be clear, so, with his heart pounding against his ribs, he darted forward onto the rocky surface. The path was hard and rough against his soft paw pads. It hurt to run across, but Shadow didn't care as long as he made it safely to the grass on the other side.

Just as his four white paws touched the soft, clover-filled grass on the other side, another swift-moving beast zoomed past. Again a gust of wind blasted him from behind, nearly knocking him off balance. Folding down his ears, Shadow squatted until the dust settled. Then Shadow let out a sigh of relief as he mentally counted how many more cats had to cross the path. Since he was now safe and sound, only seven clan members were left.

Shadow motioned with a flick of his long black tail for Tiger to join him next. Tiger nodded in understanding and trotted up to the edge of the rock path. Carefully looking in both directions, the orange tabby tom spotted a speeding beast coming quickly and decided to wait for it to pass. Dipping his head, Shadow let his friend know he agreed with his wise decision to wait. It wasn't worth risking the chance of being hit, or worse, killed.

As Tiger backed away, a small blur moved closer to the edge of the rock path. It took Shadow a few moments to realize what the tiny object was. When he did recognize what it was, his blood turned ice cold and his head swam with concern and fear. Young Milo was standing on the edge of the path.

Because the giant beast was coming fast, Shadow knew he had to stop the youngster from crossing before he went too far. The humans showed no mercy toward the Moonshine Clan in the forest. Shadow was quite sure they wouldn't make any effort to protect Milo now.

"Stop, Milo, don't come any farther! There's a beast coming toward us!" he exclaimed desperately.

The other clan members had seen the kitten as well and were now trying to get his attention. Tiger and Midnight rushed out to get the youngster, but it was too late. Milo had already stepped out onto the rough, rocky surface. They couldn't do anything except watch in horror as Milo scampered across the path.

Young Milo was almost at the bright yellow line down the middle when the beast reached him. Slowing down, the giant beast let out an earsplitting noise as it swerved in an attempt to avoid crushing Milo's tiny frozen body. Shadow's heart lurched and he temporarily stopped breathing. He hoped Milo was still alive, but his chance of survival was very slim.

The giant beast sped away almost as quickly as it had come. As the dust settled on the rocky surface, Shadow spotted the small kitten squatting in the middle of the path. A clamor of distressed meows came, no doubt, from Cassidy, Midnight, and the rest of the clan.

Flooding with relief, Shadow saw Milo's bright yellow eyes staring straight at him. They were filled with complete bewilderment, horror, and a lot of shock, but thankfully he was alive!

Just then, another beast headed quickly toward Milo's tiny frozen body. Panicking, Shadow knew he had to do something really fast in order to save the kit's life. The rest of the clan saw the beast headed for him as well. Cassidy suddenly dashed forward toward her son in an effort to save her precious boy. Midnight stopped her by pushing her away from the path, knowing she was much too upset to do anything without getting hurt herself.

"Milo!" she screeched in desperation as she clawed the ground in front of her. "Please let go of me, Midnight! We have to save our son! He's going to die! My baby is in danger!"

Tiger and Destiny were trying to figure out how to go get him while keeping Lily and Daisy safe, but he was actually closer to Shadow. Without thinking twice about the beast hurting or even killing himself, Shadow shot forward onto the rock path.

When he got to Milo, Shadow realized he was so stunned he was actually frozen in fear, which meant he would have to pull him to safety. Grabbing him by the scruff of his neck, Shadow started dragging the kitten out of the beast's way. Out of the corner of his eye he saw the swift-moving beast coming closer to them. Milo was heavy, so Shadow had a very hard time moving him quickly. Finally, Shadow's back paws touched the green, clover-filled grass.

Giving one last pull, Shadow somehow managed to get Milo clear of the beast's disastrous path. He covered Milo's tiny sand-colored body with his own as the beast pounded them with a gust of wind. Once the beast was gone, Shadow stood up to see if his young friend was okay. Milo pressed himself close to Shadow's body, shaking violently from the trauma.

"I'm so sorry," the kit muttered weakly. "I wasn't thinking."

Shadow gently nudged Milo with his muzzle trying to comfort the terrified youngster. He looked up in time to see Cassidy rushing across the rock path. She was closely followed by Daisy, Lily, and Midnight. Tiger and Destiny stayed behind as they waited for another beast to pass. As soon as the four of them arrived, Cassidy started covering Milo with licks and purrs of happiness while Midnight made sure the young tom wasn't hurt.

"Oh, Milo, my precious, precious baby!" she exclaimed.

"Are you alright, Son?" Midnight inquired as he touched Milo lightly with his muzzle and began to purr.

By now, Tiger and Destiny had joined them. Obviously worried about the youngster, Destiny immediately came over to show her concern.

"Is he okay?" Destiny asked.

"I think he's going to be fine," answered his mother. "Milo, what on earth was going through your head? You know you were supposed to wait for me and your dad! If it wasn't for Shadow, you wouldn't be here. We are very fortunate that you are alive. Have you said 'Thank you'?"

"Thanks," Milo proclaimed.

"You're welcome, Milo. The Creator definitely protected you because most kits probably wouldn't have made it through what you just did," Shadow replied.

"Shadow is absolutely right," Midnight added.

"I know we just went through a lot, but we had better get moving if we plan on finding a safe place to settle down before dark. I don't feel comfortable standing here in the open," declared Tiger.

Realizing Tiger was right about needing to keep going, the rest of the clan continued onward toward the village. Destiny ran to catch up with him while Midnight followed with Lily, Daisy, Cassidy, and finally Milo. Trailing behind them, Shadow thought back over what had just taken place. He couldn't help but think about the Creator protecting Milo. There was no doubt the Creator shielded the youngster from the beast and saved his life. In addition to protecting Milo, Shadow had also been given unbelievable strength as he pulled his little friend to safety. The whole episode was amazing. Glancing over at his buddy, Shadow could tell Milo felt bad. Judging by his bowed head and dragging tail, Milo was obviously feeling guilt for his actions. Deciding to help him forgive himself, Shadow got an idea.

"Milo, come walk with me," he suggested.

When Milo dropped his pace to walk by his side, Shadow started strutting like they did before. Milo smiled.

Chapter Eight

Sharp claws prodded Shadow into the waking world. He opened his eyes to Milo's hopeful face. Groaning, he tried to turn over and go back to sleep; however, the youngster was determined to prevent him from doing so. This time he used his muzzle to nudge Shadow again.

"Are you going out hunting today, Shadow? Would it be okay if I went with you? Momma said I could go. I just have to stay with you and away from those rock paths," the youngster blurted out excitedly.

Shadow yawned while struggling to a sitting position. He was still sore from the long journey.

"Well, I wasn't planning on hunting right this minute, but I guess we could go," Shadow remarked.

"Come on, Shadow!" Milo begged.

"Okay, Milo, I'm coming. Why are you in such a hurry?" Shadow implied.

Milo's expression changed from enthusiasm to anxiousness. Pawing the ground with his unsheathed claws, he mumbled an answer.

"Well, Dad sort of wants me to go with him. He said he wanted to teach me the fundamentals, whatever that means. Right now Dad's out hunting with Tiger, but I don't really want to go with him. He expects me to be a perfect hunter when I'm not. Plus, I'm still in trouble for the path thing so he doesn't trust me. Truthfully I would rather go with you, Shadow. You don't pressure me, and well, you understand the way I feel," he proclaimed.

Shadow was touched and honored to know Milo looked up to him more than his own father. He had no idea Milo felt this way, but it made sense. After all, Milo probably didn't remember the forest or the many things he and his dad did when he was little. Secretly, Shadow felt the same way about their relationship. However, he knew he would only hurt the father-son relationship if he told Milo. Now wasn't the time to bring up his deep affection for him when Milo's relationship with his dad was so rocky.

I'm the one who carried him all day throughout our journey here, Shadow considered. *Milo and his sisters were so young when we left. No wonder he looks up to me with so much respect!*

"Milo, Midnight loves you. I know you don't remember, but back in the forest Midnight stayed constantly with you and your sisters. He hardly ever ventured from the camp. When we left the forest we became close, because I carried you. We spent almost a half a moon together so of course we are friends. Your father just wants to be closer to you, but he doesn't know how to start. It's important for you to meet him halfway, Milo. As far as going on a hunting trip, I guess it would be okay," Shadow declared.

Grinning broadly Milo replied, "Great! Let's go before Dad gets back from hunting with Tiger. Mom said she and Destiny were going sightseeing with Lily and Daisy. They won't be back for a while either."

Shadow gave his young friend a nod of understanding. Taking the lead, he and Milo trotted out of camp matching each other's steps perfectly. They made their way out of their makeshift camp. It was actually a small hole in the ground covered by a giant mound of fallen logs. Although it wasn't exactly what Shadow had in mind for a place to live, at least it kept out the wind and springtime rain. The clan had found it several days ago when they first came to the village. Their new camp was extremely close to a human's shelter. Thankfully, the Moonshine Clan had been able to come and go unnoticed.

As the two best friends trooped on to their destination, they were greeted by a raw, breezy wind. Shadow shivered as he instantly tasted fresh kill, which made him feel grateful. It was wonderful to be able to find enough food for the entire clan to eat their fill without having to worry where the next meal would come from. Life was really starting to get better!

Now out in the open fields, Milo looked up at Shadow as if to say he was going to follow his lead. Shadow felt both strange and excited to have the chance to spend time alone with the youngster. He realized this was the first time the two of them had spent any time with each other. Skirting the small wooded area behind the human shelters, Shadow walked with Milo beside him.

The village was such a vast and complex place. It was impossible to explore the whole thing without venturing too far from their camp. Shadow concluded this place was infested with humans and their young, wild, and noisy kits. He also noticed their pampered kitty cats and their humongous, cat-eating dogs. Shadow didn't know what to think of them, but he despised the dogs' smell and their vicious snapping teeth. One thing was for sure, he definitely planned on staying far away.

Before long Shadow and Milo came to a giant field of strange-looking trees. The trees were different from anything Shadow had ever seen. Although none of them were the same height, they each shared the same odd, triangular shape. The trees sort of smelled like the pine trees back in the forest. However, the forest never had any pines shaped like these trees, so Shadow was unsure of what they were called and what kind of animals lived nearby.

As Shadow guided young Milo through the towering, triangular trees, he picked up a strong scent of mice. Twitching his ears, he sent a warning signal to let the youngster know he needed to be silent and still. Then Shadow crouched down, letting his black belly fur touch the ground. His senses told him a mouse was hidden near the trunk of the nearest tree. Slowly creeping forward, Shadow waited until the plump mouse was in sight.

Carefully getting ready to make his move, he hoped Milo wouldn't make a beginners' mistake like stepping on a twig or a dried leaf. With his claws extended, Shadow pounced on top of the small brown-furred mouse. He quickly sunk his teeth into the very surprised mouse, finishing it off.

As the warm blood spilled into his mouth, he felt blessed to have something to eat. Up until recently, Shadow never realized how essential fresh kill was. Once the mouse had finished squirming, Shadow brought it back to where Milo was standing and carefully buried it.

"Wow, that was incredible! How did you do it, Shadow? You have to tell me your secrets to hunting. It's amazing how easy you make it look," Milo demanded in a thrilled voice.

"Oh, it's definitely not easy! There are no secrets or magical things to do. In order to succeed you need a lot of skills and plenty of patience," Shadow replied, leading Milo deeper into the maze of trees.

It wasn't long before Shadow picked up the scent of another brown-furred mouse searching for bugs nearby. This time to his surprise, Milo alerted him before he could point it out.

"There is a mouse by the second tree trunk on the right," the young tom whispered, nodding in its direction. "I have never killed anything before. Do you think I could try it? Come on, I have seen you, Dad, and Tiger hunt lots of times. Just give me a chance. Please, please, let me do it."

Shadow didn't know what to do. Milo was right; he had watched the older toms hunt lots of times, but was he ready? He hadn't been weaned long, and then there was the issue with his parents.

Cassidy probably wouldn't care, but Midnight would be furious if I taught him, Shadow evaluated. *Especially the part about Milo going against his will by asking me to take him. On the other paw, I do have more patience than he does, so Milo might listen better and learn more from the experience. Besides, will it really matter if he goes hunting with me first?*

"Okay, Milo, you can give it a try; however, learning the fundamentals is an essential part of the technique of hunting. Even if you happen to kill the mouse, Midnight still has the right as your dad to teach you how to hunt his way. At least, this will get out the first-time jitters. Deal?" he proclaimed.

"Deal!" exclaimed Milo excitedly.

"Always start by scenting the air for anything edible or dangerous. Next, you will need to pinpoint the exact location of the kill in the process of crouching down. Then slowly creep forward while preparing to pounce on your target. When you get close enough, jump on him and bite down on the back of his neck. Afterward you can bury it so that other animals won't eat your kill while you continue to hunt. That's it—the fundamentals of hunting," Shadow explained.

Visibly thrilled with excitement, Milo started to follow out Shadow's instructions. Just when the young tom was getting into position, Shadow spotted something on the opposite side of the tree trunk. Seeing it was a black snake, he immediately nudged Milo with his muzzle to get his attention without scaring the mouse or causing the snake to attack.

"What am I doing wrong?" Milo inquired quietly, clearly not seeing the dangerous black snake.

"Nothing. I saw a snake over there by that tree. Don't make any fast movements. Some snakes are venomous, which means their fangs have poison. When they bite you the poison can leave you in extreme pain or can even lead to death," Shadow warned the youngster.

"Oh, yeah, I can see the snake. Don't you think he has spotted us by now? I mean, we are pretty close to him. Wouldn't it be smarter to back away to a safer location?" Milo whispered in confusion.

"No, snakes can't see things like we do. They sense their surroundings by sticking their forked tongues out. By moving you will let him know you are nearby. Let's wait to see what he will do. Perhaps he will go away. If he does come this way we'll move fast," Shadow informed him.

After waiting a while the long black snake finally slithered away from them. As soon as he was out of sight, Shadow gave Milo a nod to continue with his first hunt. Luckily it didn't take long to locate the mouse, which hadn't gone far. It was still eating some bugs at the base of another tree. Shadow was surprised the snake didn't eat the mouse by swallowing it whole.

Bending down, the youngster carefully tiptoed forward until he was within killing distance. He raised his haunches, shook them once, and awkwardly dove onto the squealing mouse. After several inexperienced attempts, the young tom finally managed to kill him. When the hunt was over, Milo picked up his prey and proudly carried the mouse to Shadow.

"Well, how was your first kill? Was it anything like you had imagined?" Shadow asked with a smile.

"Seeing the snake was very scary. It gave me the chills. I'm so glad you spotted him before I got too close. The hunt was okay, but as strange as it sounds it was sort of sad at the same time. For some reason I can't stop thinking about those pitiful beady eyes staring at me. I was scared of messing up, but considering it was my first time I think I did well. Thanks for teaching me," he replied.

"Unfortunately killing mice and other animals is something we cats do in order to survive. Although it seems harsh, it's the way the Creator made us. Sometimes we pursue our prey, and sometimes we are the ones being hunted down. It all comes down to killing other animals for survival and not for enjoyment or violence. The main thing is to always be thankful for whatever food we do get and only kill other animals as food or for our protection," Shadow commented.

"Mom has been teaching the three of us a lot about the Creator since I crossed the rock path. It's interesting to know the Creator made animals different. We eat meat, but mice eat worms and bugs. He must be pretty smart to have created everything in the whole world. I mean, He made the trees, flowers, sun, moon, mountains, and of course us," Milo pointed out.

Shadow chuckled, "Yes, the Creator is awesome. He has a plan for all of us, too."

Milo didn't say anything else as he picked up the limp mouse. As Shadow unburied his own mouse and grabbed it in his jaws, he reflected on his first hunting experience many moons ago. To the best of his knowledge it was also a mouse, although the only detail he remembered of the occasion was those same beady eyes Milo described earlier. Oddly enough the aspect of killing another animal had bothered him as a youngster as well, but he had gotten over it knowing it was at least something to eat.

Thinking about Milo's first hunt made Shadow feel so proud. It felt both rewarding and gratifying to have taught the young tom something useful and worthwhile. Hopefully, Milo wouldn't have such a hard time killing his next prey since they had discussed survival skills.

Walking side by side, the two best friends headed back to the log-covered headquarters. When they were nearly there an uncomfortable prickle went down Shadow's spine. Shivering, he remembered having the same troubling feeling back in the forest when he first noticed the humans were changing the area. The sensation had been a sign from the Creator that something bad was going to happen.

Looking nervously around the clearing, Shadow searched their surroundings for any dangers or threats and scented the air for unusual scents. Nothing out of the ordinary came to him, and everything seemed quiet except for some barking dogs in the distance.

Trembling, Shadow tried to shake the awful feeling while reminding himself there was a chance he was totally overreacting. Deep down in his soul he felt like the Creator was warning him of possible trouble ahead. What kind of trouble he and his friends were in for, he wasn't sure. Shadow only hoped his feelings were wrong.

Chapter Nine

Survival in the Moonshine Clan's new home wasn't easy. Between the humans and their pesky dogs, the clan had a hard time settling down into the fast-paced village life.

Earlier, Shadow had been chased by two dogs. To begin with, the big, long-haired brown dog was the only one hunting him. As a noise erupted from inside a shelter with huge, shiny red beasts and long, snakelike objects, Shadow saw another dog join the chase. This dog was tall and had a white coat with black spots. On his head he wore a bright red object similar to the ones his humans had on as they boarded their red beasts and took off, making their noise and forcing all the other beasts to stop.

Strangely the two dogs seemed more interested in chasing the red beasts and finally left Shadow alone. Thinking he was safe, Shadow quit running to catch his breath. Looking around at the area to see where he was, Shadow realized he accidentally ran into the center of a place where four rock paths connected. Hanging above him were several objects that changed colors from green to yellow to red. This miraculously told the swarm of beasts to stop one way and go another.

To his horror the beasts began to blow their earsplitting noise and lurched at him from two different directions. Running from them, he was chased by another beast and barely missed being squashed by one turning in front of him. Escaping this near-death incident and being totally exhausted, Shadow decided it was time to forget hunting and go home.

After returning, Shadow shared his horrifying experience with his friends. It was decided the clan would stay away from that part of the village for now. Thankfully the remaining afternoon had gone by relatively quietly as Shadow volunteered to occupy the kits by playing games.

By now, the cream-colored moon was almost at its highest. Tonight, the bright ball seemed to light up everything around the small clearing. While sitting with the rest of the clan, he gazed up at its magnificent shape. Shadow recalled the last time he saw the full moon.

No one could have guessed this would be our fate, he reflected. *There's probably nothing left of our forest home. Oh, well, maybe we can finally get our life together. I wish I could stop having this same uneasy feeling, though. If I didn't know better I would say we were being watched.*

"Shadow," Milo blurted out, breaking into Shadow's private thoughts. "Can you please tell us a story about the forest? What was it like before the humans took it away from us?"

Noticing Daisy and Lily had perked up at this suggestion, Shadow put his own concerns aside. All three kits loved to hear stories about their old forest home. To Shadow's surprise, Cassidy and Destiny also sat up to listen. Even Midnight and Tiger turned their ears in his direction, although they pretended otherwise.

Forgetting his worries, Shadow began to tell the story about their home in the blackberry bush. Describing the camp, he guided the youngsters through the maze of birch and oak trees. He mentioned the protective branches of the giant maple in the center of the woods. Then, he told them about the fields surrounding the forest. Shadow even remembered the faraway mountaintops standing tall against the horizon.

Even though telling the kittens about the forest helped soothe the pain, Shadow knew what part came next. Unfortunately there was no way to give them the real story without mentioning the reason they were now living in their makeshift camp on the edge of the village. With a heavy heart, he started to relay the events leading up to the humans taking over their home.

"So, that brings us up to this point of our journey. The Creator led us here with the goal to stay together and raise you as true forest cats," he finished.

Shadow noticed the adult she-cats wore horrified looks while they recalled the terrible events. Tiger was staring off into the darkness, as if he was looking at the wrecked forest. However, Midnight had his eyes on his three kits. Shadow felt sure he was remembering how scarce the food had been.

Suddenly without any warning, a dark shape came within view, totally catching the clan off guard. Shadow wasn't sure how long the shadow had been there, but as the shape came closer he realized it belonged to a cat. Flicking his black tail as a signal to his friends he watched in amazement as not one but six visitors came out from the darkness. Seeing their company coming closer, Shadow took his place between Midnight and Tiger while Destiny and Cassidy moved protectively in front of the kittens.

The Moonshine Clan had never come in contact with any other cats. Considering these had snuck up on them, it didn't appear like they were very friendly. All of the six guests seemed to be following one cat in particular. He had long, silver-gray fur with a vicious look on his face. The cats stopped before the clan and spread out, revealing three more toms and two she-cats.

"Well, well, well, who do we have here? I don't believe we have met before," proclaimed the silver-gray tom, smirking wickedly.

"I know we haven't. Who do you think you are?" Tiger countered sharply as his orange tabby fur rose in opposition to the obvious authority the other tom held.

"I am, Bombay, the self-appointed leader of the gang," the scarred tom announced arrogantly.

"Being the second in command, I'm Bengal," declared the brown, spotted tom on Bombay's left.

The dark tabby on Bombay's right spoke next: "I'm Devon, and this is Pixie."

As he spoke, he flicked his long tail toward an orange, black, and white calico she-cat, who was standing next to him.

"This is Scarlet, and I'm Orie," stated a light brown tom beside Bengal.

He swished his tail at the she-cat named Scarlet. Once the group had stated their names, their leader, Bombay, stepped forward.

"So, who are you supposed to be? I don't remember meeting any of you before or giving you permission to live here," the leader declared.

Immediately Midnight spoke up in a forceful tone of voice, "First of all, our clan does not need to have anyone's permission to do anything. The Creator has given us the freedom to live wherever we choose. To answer your question, my name is Midnight. This is Tiger and Shadow."

"I see. Well, since you're new around here, I'll let that comment slide. As far as this Creator you speak of, He has no authority. This place is our private territory, and my laws apply to anyone within our boundaries. So far, your clan has taken food and has claimed our area as your own. I don't know where you came from, but there are two choices. First choice, you can join our gang and respect our ways. Or second, you can go back to where you came from," Bombay replied angrily.

"What!" exclaimed Tiger furiously. "We never stole any of your territory or food! There is no way you can force us to follow your so-called rules. We are not leaving just because you said so, and we are definitely not joining your gang."

"Oh, but you have stolen food. You see anything you kill and eat inside our territory is considered stealing because I did not give you permission to do so. We have been keeping an eye on you for a while now. Just a few days ago, Devon and Orie watched Shadow among the trees hunting. After killing the mouse, you showed young Milo how to hunt," proclaimed Bombay.

At this comment, Shadow was completely shocked. Midnight hadn't mentioned Milo's name to these cats. The only way they could have known would be if they were close enough to hear their conversation. A chill went down his spine, the same sensation he had been having. This wasn't good;

these cats looked hostile, and Tiger had just made matters worse. The leader, Bombay, gave his wicked smile. He knew he had scared the clan.

"Since you aren't going to join our gang, you have until the full moon is the highest in the sky to leave. Afterward, we better not find you in our territory. If we do, you will be either tortured severely or given the most painful and humiliating death you can imagine. Actually, you're lucky. I could kill you now in front of these precious kits," Bombay said.

Then just as quickly as the wicked gang had appeared, they slipped back into the shadows, completely unnoticed.

Midnight was the first to speak up in a furious tone, "Milo, you went hunting with Shadow? I told you I was going to teach you! No wonder you didn't want to go with me the other day. You said you were tired!"

Shadow really didn't think now was the time to question Milo. The hunting situation was nothing compared to being murdered by some rogue cats. Luckily, Shadow didn't have to discuss the matter or try to convince Midnight the hunt was the least of his problems because Tiger interrupted.

"Right now it's not important to know what happened between Milo and Shadow. We have to decide what to do and act upon the choice we make. There are too many of those cats to fight with the kittens, so we probably wouldn't last long if we stayed to fight them," he advised.

"Fine, but once we find a safe place to hide I want to have some answers, Milo," Midnight stated bitterly.

Shadow could tell Midnight wasn't happy, and deep down he couldn't blame him. After all, he was struggling to keep Milo under control. Somehow he already knew this would happen; however, he had dismissed his good sense and went along with Milo anyway. What was he thinking?

"Well," Shadow began hesitantly as he avoided Midnight's nasty gaze, "all of us know going back wouldn't be smart because there probably aren't any trees left. I guess the best thing to do is to travel to the other side of the village. Perhaps we can find some kind of shelter there."

Everyone nodded, although Tiger and Midnight both looked doubtful.

"Let's hurry. Those cats obviously mean what they say. It gives me the creeps to know they have been watching us so closely. No one mentioned Milo's name, so they must have been close enough to hear us talk," declared Destiny as she started to walk briskly into the night.

Tiger surprisingly trotted next to Destiny, matching her every step. Midnight went next with Cassidy, Daisy, and Lily following. Milo brought up the end with Shadow. However, the youngster never looked up at him, mainly because his father was watching his every move.

As the clan traveled swiftly through the multitudes of humans' shelters, Shadow noticed the bright cream-colored moon was nearly at its peak. Shadow knew he and his friends didn't have long before they became the prey. This thought alone made him shiver with horror. Just then, he heard a dog barking. The noise seemed to get louder and louder. Out of the shadows, a black-furred dog emerged with his vicious teeth snapping wildly.

The entire Moonshine Clan took off madly through the maze of trees and shelters. Shadow could feel his heart beating rapidly against his ribs. He hoped the ferocious dog wouldn't catch up to them, but he knew he and his friends were still weak from the long trip from the forest.

Up ahead, Shadow saw the clan would have to cross a rock path. The beasts were zooming by so fast he knew they had no chance of survival.

All of a sudden, a thought struck him, one that would save them from their deadly situation. He sped up, charging in front of Milo, Midnight with the she-cats, and finally in front of Tiger and Destiny.

"Come on, guys, follow me. I have an idea," he declared through gasps of breath.

While exploring with Midnight and Tiger several days ago, the three of them had discovered some sort of cave on the rock paths. Rain water went down into them, so the rock paths wouldn't flood and wash the human beasts away. The opening was just big enough for a cat to squeeze into. Shadow only hoped the clan could get inside before it was too late.

As Shadow came to the path, he quickly dove into the draining cave.

He landed on a small, hard surface not far from the opening. Milo skidded into the cave next, followed by his two sisters. Cassidy and Destiny pushed themselves in almost at the same time. Then Midnight came sliding in with Tiger on his tail.

Just as Tiger entered, they heard the roar of a beast above them. It must have frightened the dog, because he no longer tracked them down. Shadow looked around to see that everyone was exhausted and flustered.

Once the Moonshine Clan was safe, the toms took a look around the draining cave. It was dark with human objects strewn everywhere. The cave went two different ways seemingly following the rock path up above them. Thankfully no other animals appeared to live here, which meant they were safe for the time being.

"This place looks safe, so we might as well stay here for the night. Hopefully those evil cats won't find us down here or that vicious barking dog," Tiger reflected.

"We had better get some sleep in case they do find us and we have to run away again," advised Cassidy, giving Midnight a look to leave Milo alone for the night.

She curled herself on the edge of the flooring, while Daisy and Lily curled up beside her. Midnight laid down on the edge and started to groom Cassidy's fur. Tiger lay opposite of Midnight, forming a circle around the kits.

To Shadow's complete amazement, Destiny rested her head along Tiger's flank. She brushed her fluffy white fur onto his orange. Shadow took his place between the two toms, as Milo rested his head against him. He knew Midnight was watching and probably wasn't exactly happy.

When Shadow was almost asleep, Milo asked a question, "Shadow, what happens to us in your story?"

Shadow didn't have an answer to this, so he replied, "I don't know, Milo. I just don't know. The Creator will take care of us."

Chapter Ten

Wincing, Shadow licked his sore paw pads. Ever since the encounter with the vicious-looking gang, the clan was secretly making their way to the other side of the village. Sometimes they ventured outside, but mostly they traveled through the underground caves. Staying inside the protected caves, they were able to remain hidden from the gang and the dogs.

Shadow had been amazed by the way the caves connected to one another. All the clan had to do was follow the underground tunnel to the next exit, which always led to the rock paths above them. Although he wasn't exactly sure where they were, at least they were alive.

Unfortunately, the evil gang failed to mention how far their territory extended, which was probably on purpose. Therefore, the Moonshine Clan had no choice but to continue living like outlaws. Shadow desperately yearned for the spongy moss bed back in the forest. Even the fallen leaves in the log cave slept better than the hard, rough surface of the draining caves.

On top of this, the clan soon found out how horrible a rainstorm actually was. Sleeping in the caves during a downpour meant a completely sleepless night as they were greeted by a waterfall of rain pouring down from the rock paths above them. In addition, all sorts of human objects came down with the rain. Talk about being wet!

Shadow was beginning to wonder if the rainbow to their problems would ever come. He thought moving to the village would end the madness of the humans and thus make their lives happier. However, despite the fact the humans were no longer an issue, the situation with the gang proved much worse than their previous hardships.

Being chased like criminals wasn't what Shadow had in mind. He couldn't see the harm in finding food or shelter, but these cats weren't the type you could persuade or reason with. After all, what kind of cat would be willing to kill its own kind if they didn't obey? It was obvious the gang didn't honor or love the Creator like they did.

Yesterday afternoon, the clan wasn't lucky enough to catch anything in the small amount of time they had to hunt before sunset. This meant they would have to go out again this morning for some fresh kill. Shadow really did not want to go because he was exhausted from not getting enough sleep. Nonetheless, he told Midnight and Tiger he would, knowing how dangerous it was to hunt in broad daylight. They needed extra sets of eyes to look for the gang since they still didn't know where the boundaries were.

Sighing, Shadow licked his right paw and pushed it over his ears and face to clean up a little and refresh himself. Just as he had finished grooming, his young friend Milo came up to him.

"When are you guys going hunting, Shadow?" he questioned.

Midnight approached them before Shadow could answer, "Milo, you will be going with us today. It's too dangerous for all three of you kits to go, but you seem to be the eager one. You must obey me completely and do exactly what I say. Do you understand?"

Shadow was surprised. This was the first time anything had been said about the hunting situation. Clearly, Midnight hadn't forgiven Milo for hunting with him. Evidently Cassidy must have kept Midnight from mentioning it until now.

"Yes, Dad, I do," Milo answered sharply.

Cringing, Shadow knew Midnight wouldn't take Milo's disrespectful tone lightly. He felt the youngster was only making the circumstances worse. With a look at his son, Midnight turned around and climbed out of the cave into the daylight. Once he was gone, Shadow spoke up.

"Milo, you have to meet your dad halfway. You can't allow your feelings to get in the way. He needs to know how much pressure you're under to please him. Just try to show him respect and listen carefully to what he says. I know you are nervous, but don't worry. You'll do fine, and I will be there supporting you and cheering you on," Shadow advised.

The youngster gave him a reluctant nod of understanding as the two of them climbed up out of the draining cave and into the warm sunlight. Considering it was still early, Shadow could tell it was going to be a hot day with hardly any breeze at all. Between the increasing heat and the prolonged days, Shadow knew summer was finally here. The trees were now full of nice big, green leaves and the food was plentiful. Although, they were close to the humans' shelters, the clan usually got by unnoticed, though admittedly they weren't normally out in the sun for long.

As he and Milo trotted after Midnight and Tiger, Shadow scented the air for any dangers. Thankfully he didn't see or taste anything out of the ordinary. Then he instantly tasted a mouse and pinpointed it to a yellow bell bush nearby. The other toms had obviously scented the mouse as well, for they stopped near the bush. Midnight then turned to look at Milo.

"Okay, Milo, this one's yours. First you have to —," he began.

"I know what I'm doing, Dad. Just give me a chance to prove myself. Meet me halfway on this, please," interrupted Milo.

Shadow noticed Milo looked his way when he asked his father to meet him halfway. He knew Milo was really trying to cooperate, which took guts, considering he inherited his father's proud genes.

He realized it would be rather hard for a father or son to give in to each other. Shadow just hoped they not only gained the other's respect but could also forge the kind of relationship that both deserved.

Without waiting for his father's response, Milo dropped into the hunter's crouch, took aim, and pounced onto the mouse, quickly finishing it off without much of a struggle. Once the young tom was done, he brought his kill back to his father while Shadow watched proudly.

"Well, Dad, what did you think? I know I probably didn't do it exactly like you wanted me to, but I gave it my all. I wanted to hunt with Shadow first, because I thought I wasn't good enough. I was wrong and I'm sorry. It's just you expect me to be perfect and I'm not. Shadow isn't my dad. He only wanted to help me, like I asked him to. We'll always have a special relationship, but Shadow's right: you and I do, too. I hope you can forgive me," Milo declared.

"Of course I do, Milo. I'm the one who should be sorry. I never knew you felt this way. No, you aren't perfect, but who is? As for our relationship, I think it could use some help. Maybe Shadow could teach you to pay attention and teach me how to be patient," Midnight replied smiling.

Shadow smiled, too, as he was happy to know neither of them had hard feelings. Tiger, who was sitting beside Shadow and listening to the conversation, now got up. He obviously didn't like being a part of the sentimental discussion.

"Hurry, we don't need to be spotted," he stated firmly as he trotted off.

After the toms caught a feathered titmouse, a sparrow, and two more mice, they made their way to the she-cats. Once they arrived at their secret hideout, the toms filed one by one down into the draining cave on the edge of the rock path. As they entered, Shadow heard Daisy and Lily's high-pitched screams echoed throughout the cave.

"What on earth is going on?" Midnight blurted out in surprise.

No sooner had the words came out of his mouth that Shadow saw what was happening. While Milo's sisters panicked on one side of the cave, their mother and Destiny were hissing and fighting something in the opposite direction. From where he stood, Shadow could tell they were jointly attacking a humongous wolf rat. To his amazement the two she-cats managed to kill their attacker, which was nearly as big as they were. Finally finishing him off, Cassidy turned around to see if her girls were okay. As she did so, she spotted the toms.

"Are you alright?" Midnight asked as he went over to her.

"Yes, we are now. For a while there I didn't think Destiny and I were going to kill that rat. He was huge!" Cassidy related, sighing with relief.

"Yeah, he was definitely the toughest thing I have ever killed. He snuck up on us and was trying to harm the girls. He actually had a pretty firm grip on Lily, but between the two of us we saved her," Destiny explained.

Midnight immediately approached his daughter, "Did he hurt you, Lily?"

"I'm okay, but it was very scary. It was the biggest mouse I have ever seen in my whole life!" she proclaimed, giving her dad a hug.

Chuckling, Midnight replied, "He's not really a mouse, sweetheart. He's a wolf rat, which is sort of related to mice. I still believe he's the biggest rat any of us have seen."

While they had been talking, Shadow hadn't noticed Milo was no longer standing by his side. Looking around he realized Milo's curiosity had gotten the best of him. The youngster was now standing over the dead wolf rat. Standing beside the creature he appeared small.

"Wow," Milo breathed, "this wolf rat is gigantic. He is so ugly. Look at his fangs and those claws. Do you reckon his fangs are poisonous like the snake's are?"

Shadow joined his young friend, "No, I don't think they carry poison, but he could probably tear you up if he got a good hold on you. Thank goodness your mom and Destiny saved Lily and Daisy in time."

"Are we going to eat him?" Milo wanted to know.

"No, they eat a lot of disgusting things, most of which are rotten. If we eat him we might get a sickness and die. We should probably drag him farther down the draining cave," Shadow answered.

"The other day I found an opening in the cave where it dumped out into a field of grass. Perhaps we could leave him there for the buzzards to eat. Those huge birds will pretty much eat anything," Tiger commented.

Nodding in agreement, Shadow helped Tiger drag the huge wolf rat down the right side of the cave. The rat was heavy, but between the two of them they managed to pull it to the far end of the cave. After quite awhile of pulling, Shadow finally saw the opening Tiger had described. Yanking the rat a little farther, they dropped his heavy body and left him for the buzzards.

By the time Shadow and Tiger returned, Destiny, Cassidy, Midnight, and the kits were in the process of splitting up the fresh kill they had caught. Settling down to eat the Moonshine Clan thanked the Creator and quickly devoured the fresh kill.

Just as the cats finished eating, a noise sounded above them. Shadow looked up with everyone else. As he did so, he found himself looking straight into the face of a dark gray cat. Shadow could tell by its smell it was a tom and he wasn't alone.

"I thought I heard someone talking. What are you doing down there? Come out here where we can see you better," declared the tom.

Suddenly Shadow felt sick to his stomach. As if the day hadn't been stressful enough, now they had company. The tom didn't look like any from the gang, but then again he really didn't pay attention to the details of their appearances because of the darkness.

Regretfully, Shadow followed Tiger and the rest of the clan out into the sunlight and into the presence of the cats. He felt thankful that neither Tiger nor Midnight had challenged these cats and hoped they remained on their best behavior. When the Moonshine Clan and the other five cats had gathered beneath a nearby low-lying bush, the gray furred tom began to speak.

"Alright, look. I don't know where your little group came from, but we don't want you here," he said forcefully.

"That's right, just leave and don't come back! We don't want any trouble," exclaimed the dark brown tom beside him.

"Wait a minute," proclaimed a black and white she-cat. "I'm sorry for my clan mate's rudeness. We usually don't have many strange cats in our territory. My name is Angel. What's yours?"

She gave her fellow clan members a sharp look as if to say they needed to be polite. Oddly they seemed to listen to her, which made Shadow wonder why.

"Okay, okay, we get the idea. I'm Tonk and this is Marcus," muttered the gray tom, as he pointed at the brown one with his tail tip.

Beside him the silver-blue she-cat spoke, "I'm Abigail, and this is Lena."

As the first she-cat spoke, the light gray she-cat on her left dipped her head and gave them a smile.

"So, who are you?" Angel asked again.

Midnight and Tiger looked at each other, not sure whether they should or shouldn't tell these strange cats. Shadow decided they seemed to be friendly. So maybe in this situation someone besides Tiger needed to explain. Trying to remain humble, he spoke in a trusting voice realizing their lives depended upon the way these cats perceived his character.

"We are the Moonshine Clan. We came from a forest on the other side of this village. The humans ran us out so we came here. Then some gang of vicious cats told us we had to leave or else. That's why we are hiding; we didn't mean to intrude. Oh, I'm Shadow and this is Midnight and Tiger. The she-cats are Cassidy and Destiny, and the kits are Milo, Daisy, and Lily. We mean no harm to your clan or anyone else."

"I see. Well, the gang you speak of is the Black Widow Gang, and yes, they mean what they say. Don't worry, though; we'll take you to our base where you'll be safe. By the way, we are a part of the Village Cats. There are a large number of us, but no need to be scared," replied Angel.

"I don't know if we should take them with—," the tom named Tonk began.

Angel cut him off by flicking him roughly with her tail and giving him another nasty gaze. The two of them appeared to not be agreeing with each other, and apparently Angel's opinion won out.

"Fine. It will take us several days to reach our base, so we had better get moving," urged Tonk, as he eyed the kits wearily.

Not wasting any time, the Moonshine Clan fell in line behind the Village Cats. Shadow hoped these cats were telling the truth.

Chapter Eleven

Chilly dampness engulfed Shadow as he trotted along the edge of the woods. He and his friends had been following the five Village Cats back to their base for the last few days. By now, the rain had set in, which meant the trip would be rough. To Shadow, the bad weather matched his feelings. He wondered if their bad luck would ever change. Shadow wished the tiny flicker of hope in his heart stayed there, but he had been let down so many times he wasn't sure if it would. In his head everything seemed to be mixed up, like a wild, tangled thorn bush.

Wonder why everything has to be so complicated, he debated. *I'm very worried and trying hard not to show it.*

First, we had the big problem of the human invasion. Now encountering the Black Widow Gang and trying to survive in this village could be harder than the forest ever was. No matter how much we try, we just can't seem to fit in.

Next was the friction between Milo and Midnight, which hopefully appears to be solved for now at least. We still haven't been able to properly teach the kittens survival skills.

Then there's Tiger and Destiny. Their relationship was like the weather: it is one day sunny and the next day rainy. Neither of them could make up their minds, despite the fact they were both madly in love with each other. I don't understand why love does that to some cats.

Plus on top of all this, I have been watching Angel. She is an interesting cat. There is something about her I just can't figure out.

Shadow gazed at her as he trotted along. She was so beautiful to him. Her fur was black down her neck, back, and long tail. She had a white underbody like Daisy, but she did wear a few black splotches on her paws.

To Shadow, though, her best physical feature was her charming face. The area around her eyes and ears was black, while her chin and chest fur was white. Between her lime green eyes, she wore a white blaze and nearly always wore a big smile.

As Shadow kept pace with his friends, he couldn't help wondering what her personality was like. She seemed to be a sweet girl, but he knew this didn't mean she was one.

While he was thinking, his friends and the Village Cats decided to stop for a rest. Shadow, who had been following everyone else, was so caught up in his thoughts he didn't notice he had passed Tiger and Destiny.

He never saw Cassidy, Midnight, or the kits either. Milo called out his name, but Shadow didn't hear him. He just kept on walking with his head down lost in his private thoughts and concerns.

The Village Cats were all sitting around Angel, discussing the remaining portion of the trip. Angel had her back toward Shadow, but the other four cats saw him.

Lena and Abigail, the other she-cats, stared at him in shock. Meanwhile the toms, Tonk and Marcus, started chuckling with amusement.

Then, just like that, Shadow walked straight into Angel. Confused, Shadow shook his head to bring himself out of his dream world. Realizing what he had done, he felt his fur grow hot with embarrassment as Angel turned around.

"I-I-I'm so sorry, Angel! I guess I didn't realize we stopped. I hope you can forgive me," he stammered awkwardly.

By now everyone, including his own clan, was laughing at him. He glanced up at Angel, knowing she would now think he was crazier than a goofy, birdbrained squirrel. To his surprise, she wasn't laughing hysterically like the others. She was smiling at him, though.

"It's 'Shadow,' right?" she asked sweetly.

"Yeah, it is," he shyly answered.

"Well, Shadow, there's no need for you to feel bad. It was an accident. We're just stopping long enough to rest our paws. We are almost there actually," she proclaimed in her enchanting voice.

"Oh, okay," he muttered, as he turned around and went back to his friends.

Despite all of the kittens' questions, Shadow just sat down and waited until it was time to go again. For some reason, he just could not keep his eyes away from Angel. What was more, she remembered his name!

It wasn't long before the group of thirteen started off again. Following the woods, they came upon some tall human shelters. The group trotted through these quickly, avoiding both the humans and their barking dogs. Then, they went past these giant shelters. Angel explained the humans got their food from inside them and picked up other things as well.

Sure enough, she was right; the place was swarming with humans and their young kits. Most of their kits walked beside the adults holding their front paws; however, some of the tiny ones had to be carried. It gave Shadow an eerie feeling to be so close to these cruel creatures.

The cats walked across a huge rock path while weaving through rows of beasts lined up waiting for their humans to return. Even though the beasts weren't alive right now, it still gave Shadow the creeps to be in their presence. He wondered if they could wake up without the humans in them and decided he would rather not find out.

Thankfully the Village Cats didn't stay long in the presence of the beasts. They quickly led the Moonshine Clan down the side of the human's food shelter toward the back. Shadow noticed Milo and his sisters wore a scared look on their faces. He couldn't blame them; he was uneasy about the situation, too.

Suddenly Angel stopped and said, "Okay, you guys, this is it. Our base is right around this corner in the tall grass. You all need to stay close.

Remember, nobody here knows about any of you. No one will hurt you, of course, but we don't want to worry anyone. We'll take you to our leader; however, we have to pass a lot of cats to get to her. Just follow us."

She and her fellow clan mates led the Moonshine Clan into their base. Angel was absolutely right; there were cats everywhere. There was no way Shadow could count them all. Everyone stared at them, both confused and curious about the new arrivals. Some cats started whispering to each other and some even followed, eager to see what was going on.

When the group reached the grass, every cat parted to allow them through. Sitting in the middle of the gathered cats was a sand-colored tabby she-cat. Her hazel eyes glittered with leadership and courage as she peered at them in interest.

Shadow felt sure she must be the leader Angel had mentioned. He only hoped she would allow his clan to stay until they got stronger. Shadow knew living in the draining caves had weakened them considerably.

"Good evening, Sandy," Angel declared, dipping her head to show her leader admiration and respect.

"Good evening, Angel. What do you have here, friends or enemies?" she asked.

"As far as we know they are friends and mean no harm," Angel responded.

"We found them in the drains along the rock paths," Tonk added rudely. "They call themselves the Moonshine Clan and claim the Black Widow Gang threatened them."

"They lived in a forest, knowing nothing about our territory rights or the gang's. We brought them here for shelter and food until they get stronger," Marcus finished.

"I see, and I suppose you'll tell me your names. Then you can all go and get some rest," proclaimed Sandy.

"I'm Shadow," Shadow replied, "and these two are Midnight and Tiger. This is Destiny and Midnight's family, Cassidy, Milo, Daisy, and Lily."

"Welcome to our home," the leader answered.

She turned to the gray tabby tom with a white underbelly next to her. He clearly held an important role as well.

"Comet, get some food for these cats. Angel, take them to the den," she requested.

The tom named Comet gave her a curt nod and left. Angel proceeded to lead the clan to a nearby mountain laurel bush. There were several bushes with cats in each, apparently sleeping.

"All right, guys, this is where you will be sleeping. If there is anything you need just let one of us know and we will be happy to get it for you. I'll be back in a little while," Angel declared as she motioned with her tail for them to enter the bush.

Once Angel was gone the adult members of the Moonshine Clan sat down to discuss sleeping arrangements and the events of the last few days. Meanwhile Milo, Daisy, and Lily roamed around the bush. Having seen everything, the three of them returned to listen to the adult conversation.

"Do you think we are safe here?" Daisy blurted out in a fearful voice.

The young she-cat's question interrupted the adults, forcing them to include the three kittens in their discussion.

"Yes, dear, I think we will be safe now. The gang won't sneak up on us with so many cats, and these cats seem to know how to deal with them. There is no need for you to worry," Midnight replied lovingly.

"So we're going to live here?" Milo piped up.

At this comment Midnight hesitated before speaking, "For the time being we probably should, but we will have to discuss what we need to do next. Hopefully the Village Cats can help us figure out where everybody's so-called boundaries are and find a place of our own."

"I agree. Perhaps we can learn from the Village Cats," Shadow proclaimed.

"How are we going to sleep, Momma? I'm tired," Lily wanted to know.

Cassidy smiled at her daughter, "Come on, let's figure it out while we wait for someone to bring us something to eat."

While the Moonshine Clan was deciding how they would sleep, Marcus and Tonk entered and chose a sleeping place for themselves on the left side of bush. Lena and Abigail came in behind them and did the same, making sure to leave enough room for their company. It never occurred to Shadow and his friends that the Village Cats would be staying with them. Shadow could only assume Sandy didn't know them well enough to let them stay alone.

As Shadow, Midnight, and Tiger gave each other a confused look, Comet and a few other Village Cats brought plenty of fresh kill for all of them to eat. Dropping the food in the center of the bush, Comet left them to eat their meal. Shadow and his friends closed their eyes and gave thanks to the Creator. Then they each took a mouse and began to eat. Glancing over at the Village Cats, Shadow realized Lena, Abigail, and Marcus had their eyes closed presumably thanking the Creator in private. It didn't appear like Tonk had done so, though he could have.

Noticing Angel hadn't returned yet, Shadow considered what she was doing. As her friends began to eat their meal, Angel's black and white pelt suddenly entered the bush. Trotting up to the remaining meat, she took her mouse and went to sit with Lena and Abigail. Shadow watched her close her eyes and mutter something under her breath before eating. He figured they, unlike the gang, must have some knowledge of the Creator.

After they had eaten their delicious meal, Midnight led the way to the area on the right side of the bush, opposite of where the Village Cats were. Cassidy took her place beside him as Daisy and Lily cuddled against their mother lovingly. Tiger and Destiny chose to sleep across from them. Shadow settled on the outside of the group, with young Milo next to him.

By now, everyone had found a place to relax except for Angel. As the two groups curled up and began to drift off to sleep, she tiptoed around her friends. Without much of a choice she made her bed between her friend Lena and Shadow. When nobody was looking or listening, she leaned over and gently whispered in his ear.

"Good night, Shadow, I hope you and your friends sleep well tonight," she muttered softly.

"Maybe we will. Thanks for all you have done for us and for convincing your leader to let us stay. Good night," Shadow quietly responded.

Deep down, Shadow was very appreciative of her kind hospitality, yet he was also a little bit restless and uncomfortable having her sleep so close to him. Although it did make him feel good to know, he and his clan were safe for now. At least they had a dry place to sleep and an abundance of food. The best part of the whole situation was the fact that they didn't have to worry about being attacked by the Black Widow Gang. Here they would have a better chance of survival and could actually rest, knowing they could sleep and not be concerned for the safety of the kittens.

Curling himself into a ball, Shadow tucked his tail around Milo's sand-colored fur coat. Listening to their snoring and with one last look at his young best friend, he finally managed to drift off to sleep next to Angel.

Chapter Twelve

Right now, Shadow was headed to the Village Cats' sleeping den. Their leader, Sandy, gave him permission to go hunting, as long as he stayed close to the base. He had decided to ask Tiger to go with him, since Midnight was out teaching hunting skills with Milo.

It didn't take Shadow long to reach the bushy den. He was slowly getting used to sleeping, eating, and hunting here. Everything was so much different from what he and his friends usually did. Back in the forest, the clan always made choices together, but now everyone had to ask Sandy first. It was all very confusing to Shadow.

He passed a few cats, which he didn't know as he made his way to the center of the bushes. Shadow stopped as he caught a glimpse of Tiger's orange tabby fur.

Instantly, he opened his mouth to call out his friend's name but froze as he heard Destiny's frantic voice. Shadow knew eavesdropping wasn't the right thing to do and he felt really bad. However, before he had a chance to leave he couldn't help but hear portions of their private conversation.

"Tiger, what are you talking about? I thought we had something special between us," Destiny asked.

Shadow could tell by the strong emotion in her voice she was upset.

"We do have a special relationship, Destiny. It's just I'm not sure I am right for you. Shadow is better than me in a lot of ways. For one thing he's pretty clever," Tiger responded uncomfortably.

Completely floored, Shadow felt his jaw drop. Tiger was actually jealous of him. He didn't even have those kinds of feelings for Destiny.

"Oh, Tiger, you know I don't feel that way. Shadow will always be a close friend of mine, but nothing more. It's you I care about. I, well, I love you, Tiger," she replied awkwardly.

"I love you, too, Destiny," Tiger announced lovingly, as a purr rumbled deep in his throat.

Slowly backing up, Shadow carefully eased his way out of the bush. When he was out of earshot, he picked up his pace and headed out to hunt.

I guess I'll have to hunt alone today, Shadow calculated. *Oh, well, I'm sure they want to spend some time together while everyone is busy doing other things.*

Shadow suddenly felt a pang of envy. As soon as he felt it, he instantly pushed the feeling away. He really wanted to go hunting with Tiger since Midnight and Milo were busy. Now he would have to go by himself without anyone to talk to. With his head down and his tail dragging, Shadow trotted out of the base. Just as he was leaving, a voice sounded behind him.

"Hey, Shadow! Where are you going?"

Turning around, Shadow saw the voice belonged to Angel. Although he really didn't want to tell her he had to hunt alone, he wasn't going to lie about it. Letting out a sigh he decided to respond in a generic way.

"Out hunting," he answered nonchalantly.

"Aren't you going to wait for one of your clan mates to go with you?" she questioned him.

Obviously Angel was determined to find out what he was up to. Shadow could tell by the curiosity in her voice she wasn't going to stop asking questions until he told her what he was doing and where he planned to go.

"Well, Midnight is out hunting with Milo, Cassidy is training Lily and Daisy, and Tiger is spending time with Destiny. So that leaves me hunting alone," he explained, as casually as he could manage.

"I see. Well, would you mind if I came along? I don't have any duties until dawn. Plus if I go with you, I could take you to the river. Of course, if you want to be alone I won't bother you," she urged.

At first Shadow wanted to go alone, but as he stood there trying to figure out what to do, a thought struck him. It just might be fun to see the river with Angel. He might even find out more about her personality.

"I suppose I could use the company," he agreed, smiling.

Eagerly, Angel started off at a trot. Shadow jogged beside her, matching her every step. Once they were out of the busy base and out of the onlookers' curious gazes, Angel spoke up.

"So, Shadow, tell me about your clan," she requested.

"Well," he began, "you already know everyone."

"True, but I was wondering what they were like before I met them. You know, their real identities," she hinted.

"Okay. Let me see, I guess I'll start with Tiger. He's always jumping up to fight anything getting in his way: Midnight, humans, evil cat-killing gangs, you name it. He is starting to settle down some, though, with Destiny's help," he told her.

At this moment, Angel let out an amused meow of laughter.

Shadow continued, "Destiny has become like a sister to me. She's sweet, but can be defensive when she is challenged. Next is Midnight, he's the wisest, although he is also hardheaded and demanding. Cassidy is very kindhearted and a wonderful mother. Plus she is the only one who can change Midnight's mind on issues."

"How about the kittens?" Angel asked.

"Daisy and Lily are a lot like their mother, but when they join Milo the three get into trouble. Milo is a pawful. We are really close friends actually. On our journey here, I carried him, so that's what he remembers the most. He recently told me he looks up to me more than his father, but I helped them work out their relationship," he declared.

"Oh, Shadow, how sweet! I have seen the way you and Milo connect. So who's the leader?" she asked.

"No one. We all make our decisions together based on what we feel the Creator leads us to do," he stated.

"I never thought about the Creator leading everyone. We just do whatever

Sandy tells us to do. I know the Creator made the world with all the plants and animals, but the idea of Him actually being concerned or interested in our lives hasn't crossed my mind. No one has ever mentioned such. I'm not sure if Sandy asks the Creator for guidance or not. I haven't heard her say," Angel commented.

"Really? I assumed everybody thought the same way. Lately I have been wondering about it more because the Black Widow Gang said the Creator had no authority over them. It's good to know you at least believe He exists," Shadow replied.

"I don't know what the gang believes, but they are evil. I'm glad your clan does believe even if you do think of the Creator differently than I have been taught," Angel declared.

The two cats bypassed several human shelters and a lot of rock paths. Soon they came to a wooded area. Angel led him through tall grass to some cattails. She then turned toward Shadow.

"Here it is, just beyond these cattails," she announced, as she pushed herself through to the other side.

When Shadow saw the river, he was amazed. The current was a strong one, gushing and gurgling to who knows where. As for the width, Shadow definitely did not wish to cross it. The water itself was crystal clear. You could even see naturally smooth and polished stones beneath the surface.

Shadow opened his mouth to point out how amazingly clear the water was to Angel. However, she quickly flicked him with her tail signaling for silence. Startled by her behavior, Shadow took a step back.

"Shh, don't move, there is a beaver upstream. Do you see him?" Angel whispered, leaning closer to Shadow.

Craning his neck to get a better look, Shadow saw what Angel was looking at. Sure enough there was a furry brown creature with a slick, flat tail sitting by the river farther upstream. Watching closely, Shadow realized the beaver was gnawing down a small tree with his sharp front teeth.

"Why is the beaver eating the tree? Aren't there enough things for him to eat without trying to chew something so hard and rough? Surely he could find a mouse or grass or something more edible," Shadow wondered aloud.

"Don't be ridiculous, Shadow. Beavers don't eat mice or large trees! They eat bark or tender trees and use the bigger ones to build their homes called a dam. Most of them usually have a tunnel under the water so they can enter their homes safely," Angel pointed out as she motioned toward a structure in the water.

Peering in the direction she was pointing to, Shadow saw a humongous mound of trees piled high in the center of the river farther upstream. From what Shadow could see, the brown-furred beaver was nearly done with his amazing creation. It was interesting how the structure could possibly be dry inside while being completely surrounded by water on the outside. The Creator had made an odd creature indeed.

"Come on, let's get something to eat. We won't bother him as long as we stay up here. I don't want to get into a fight with one today. They are nasty fighters when they are protecting their young. Beavers call them kits like we do," Angel mumbled.

Shadow watched in bewilderment as Angel settled down on a rocky boulder near the water's edge. Confused and curious, Shadow started to ask why she was concentrating on the water when she had just mentioned the idea of hunting.

Before he could speak, Angel slowly raised an unsheathed paw as she studied the water with her lime-green eyes. With a swift movement of her black spotted paw, she reached down into the water and drew out a reddish-gray fish with black spots. Once Angel got the fish onto the ground, she quickly bit down on it to finish it off.

Shadow was in complete shock; he had never seen anyone kill a fish before. Although he had often tried to catch one in a nearby creek back home, he could never quite get the hang of it.

"Well, are you going to sit there or eat this tasty fish with me?" Angel questioned him, her whiskers twitching with delight.

"I will. It's just I have never had any fish before. We couldn't figure out how to catch one. Do you mind if I give thanks to the Creator first? We always do so before eating," he answered.

Angel shrugged, "Go ahead, I usually thank the Creator privately, but I don't mind doing it with you."

Shadow smiled as he closed his eyes and began, "Thank you, Mighty Creator, for this food and for my new friend. May your will be done."

Opening his eyes, Shadow noticed Angel was staring at him with a touched look on her face. Obviously trying to hide her thoughts, she quickly looked down at her kill. Splitting the meal in half, the two of them ate the reddish-gray fish. It was so incredibly delicious! While they ate, Angel explained her technique of hunting, or as she called it, fishing. She also told him the fish was called a mountain trout and could be found in almost all the rivers.

After eating the trout, the two of them headed back to the Village Cats' base. By now, the sun was starting to set in the western sky. On the way back, Angel started to ask Shadow questions about his forest home.

Shadow walked her through the towering trees and the blackberry bush, just as he had done for the kittens nearly a moon ago. He explained what the humans had done and about their long, exhausting journey to the village. From there, Shadow recounted the terrible night when the cruel Black Widow Gang had threatened them. Finally, he told her about the odd feelings he continually had and how he considered it to be a warning from the Creator. When Shadow was finished, Angel looked at him soberly.

"Wow, you sure have been through a lot. I had no idea what you and your friends had to face every day. I can't believe you could still have hope, even though there wasn't anything to live for," she declared.

"When we left the forest it was raining, but as we got to the end of our territory the Creator placed a rainbow in the sky. It seems like every storm has a rainbow, and I believe it is a reminder to have hope. Truthfully I still have an uneasy feeling about things. Sooner or later something good will hopefully happen. We just have to trust the Creator because He has a plan for us," he proclaimed.

Angel nodded thoughtfully and gave him a smile. As the two of them trotted onward toward the base, Shadow couldn't help but feel relieved. He had finally admitted his feelings and concerns to someone. Ever since Destiny had grown closer to Tiger he couldn't share his thoughts like he did before. Now he had a new friend. He hoped she would confide in him someday. Looking at her, Shadow knew she would.

Chapter Thirteen

By this time, the long, hot summer days were filled with hunting and patrols—not only for the Village Cats, but also the Moonshine Clan as well. Shadow was always busy doing something, but he seemed to somehow end up with Angel regardless.

It felt good to have someone to talk to, and as it turned out, to listen. To Shadow's delight, Angel did indeed start to explain her life in detail. She told him about her friends, who turned out to be a lot like his friends. She explained the rules and regulations of her clan, too. Having done so, she now came to him often for advice or to simply chat about the latest adventures her friends had encountered.

Right away, Shadow noticed her friend Tonk was rather jealous of their newfound friendship. However, when he mentioned it to Angel, she only laughed. She said Tonk thought she was his girl, but as far as she was concerned he would have to keep dreaming.

Shadow could tell Angel pretty much did whatever she wanted and got the things she wished for by being loyal to her leader and to her friends. He also found out how mischievous she was. She was constantly joking around and laughing, which reminded him of Milo.

Deep inside his heart, Shadow knew he found a new friend, one who could be depended on and trusted. Most importantly, he had a friend to spend time with whenever he wanted, which was a good thing since Milo had been spending a great deal of time with his dad.

Another thing about Angel was her energetic, optimistic attitude. When Shadow felt down, she always found a way to make him happy.

Shadow hoped today's hunt would be as successful as usual. He was making his way through the base, looking for Angel's magnificent black and white coat. She had promised to take him to a tree farm for hunting.

This tree farm was the same kind of pinelike trees he and Milo had discovered near the makeshift log headquarters. Angel clarified the trees were called evergreen fir trees. At a special time during the coldest part of the winter moons, the humans put the fir trees inside their shelters for entertainment. She also told him the humans lived in houses, not shelters.

When he finally found Angel, she was busily chatting with Comet, the second in command. Waiting patiently, Shadow let her finish her conversation, knowing it probably had something to do with the many duties each member of their clan had to do. In no time at all, she was ready to check out the mysterious evergreen fir trees.

"So are you ready to see the tree farm?" Angel questioned him cheerfully.

He was about to answer her, when two brown and white she-cat sisters came bounding toward them. Their frantic arrival alerted everyone in the base, which was a lot of cats. Angel's friend Lena notified her leader, Sandy, and Comet. The she-cats were gasping for breath, but Angel was able to calm them enough to see what was wrong and to find out if either of them was hurt.

"We were out hunting when we spotted the Black Widow Gang. We ran as fast as we could, but they aren't far behind us," one of them announced.

Then the other sister spoke up, "They were talking about the newcomers. Their leader said they were going to pay for their disobedience. We must get rid of those cats or we might get killed. It's not our problem, and we don't need to make it ours."

To Shadow's surprise, most of the cats around him openly agreed with the she-cats. With mumbles and yowls the group became more and more upset. Everybody suddenly wanted to get rid of him and his friends.

He noticed the rest of the Moonshine Clan had gathered along with the other cats. They all seemed to have grasped the same assumption they were no longer welcome guests.

Shadow turned toward Angel, and to his relief she wasn't pushing them like the others were. In fact she stared at her fellow clan mates in shock as if she had no idea they could be so rude and unfriendly. She seemed genuinely disturbed by their hostility and aggressive behavior.

"I will have none of this!" ordered Sandy angrily as she approached the group.

Comet, who was standing behind his leader, moved closer to the Moonshine Clan. The tom seemed ready to jump in if anyone disobeyed their leader.

Sandy continued on, "These cats are our guests and we will treat them with respect! Now, there isn't much time to prepare for the Black Widow Gang's arrival, so we must hurry to get ready for them. As much as I regret it, I'm afraid your clan must leave at once. I am not saying this because you are no longer welcome here, but because your lives depend upon your leaving."

"If you don't mind, Sandy, I would like to show the Moonshine Clan a safe route toward the mountains," Angel requested.

"Splendid, but only take them as far as the river's bend. Then come back, just in case the gang decides to attack us," she advised.

"We'll go for protection, Angel," Tonk announced bluntly as he flicked his tail toward Marcus, Lena, and Abigail and gave the Moonshine Clan a distasteful look.

As if this small gesture was a command, they quickly followed Tonk out of the base. Angel went next, closely followed by Tiger and Destiny. Midnight, Cassidy, and the kits succeeded them, and finally Shadow.

Before leaving, Shadow called out to Sandy and Comet, "Thank you so much for everything you've done for us!"

"You are welcome. Good-bye and good luck," replied the tabby leader.

Without another word, the group trooped hastily out of the base and around the gigantic human shelter. Dodging frozen beasts lined up waiting for their humans, the thirteen cats moved swiftly. No one spoke, but Shadow knew what his clan mates were feeling: anger, sorrow, and dread—anger, for the way some of the Village Cats had treated them; sorrow, for having to leave what friends and shelter they did have; and dread, for the next harsh journey to the mountains they were about to undertake.

How come all this is happening to us? he wondered. *Why won't the Black Widow Gang just leave us alone so we can get on with our lives? It's not fair for us to always have to run away, but we don't have a choice if we want to survive. If they keep on hunting us down, we won't have anywhere else to go. Please help us, Mighty Creator!*

Looking up, Shadow realized the Village Cats and his friends were now gathered at a fence. Gazing around, he noticed it was rather long and quite high. At first he didn't understand how they were going to jump over it with the kittens; however, Marcus cleared things up.

"All right," declared Marcus, "we don't usually go under this fence because of the easier way around. In this particular situation, those cats might come after you. This way, they will follow your scents to this fence and hopefully be forced to slow up, giving you more time to escape."

Without waiting for a response, Marcus went over to a hole that went under the fence. The hole was just large enough for a full-grown cat to go under, although they would still have to squeeze through.

Before Shadow knew it, the dark tabby tom was on the opposite side of the fence and Tonk was right behind him. Abigail's silver-blue body went next, closely followed by Lena's light gray one.

The Village Cats had clearly done this before. Even Angel thrust herself underneath like it wasn't a big deal. To Shadow, this was a very big deal, and he wasn't so sure he could get enough traction to go under without getting stuck. How unfortunate it would be to get caught under it.

At this point, Tiger and Midnight looked at each other, not sure who should go first. Even though no words were exchanged between them, it seemed obvious Midnight would go. He approached the fence determinedly, ducked his head, and shoved himself under. After the solid black tom was on the opposite side, he turned to his three kittens.

"Come on, kits. Milo, you come first. Daisy will go next, and Lily will follow you," Midnight ordered.

Shadow watched as the three kittens scrambled under the fence to join their father. Cassidy followed closely, pushing them along with her muzzle.

"You go next, Destiny. I'll be right behind you," Tiger urged.

"Me? Oh, no, I can't possibly go under there, I'll get stuck!" she exclaimed, backing up and shaking her head vigorously.

"I can't believe this. She's running for her life, for goodness sakes," Tonk muttered under his breath.

Marcus snickered at his sarcastic remark, but Angel eyed the two of them sharply, obviously upset with Tonk. Shadow looked over at Tiger and Destiny. He knew if Destiny didn't get angry, Tiger would. Luckily, neither of them, Midnight, nor Cassidy seemed to notice what Tonk had said.

While Shadow was pondering on whether anyone heard the comment, Tiger finally coaxed Destiny into going under the fence. She crouched down to go beneath it, but when she was halfway her fluffy white fur got caught. This caused her to go into a panic attack. Shadow couldn't believe his thoughts actually came true.

"Oh no, Tiger, help me please!" she pleaded desperately.

"Don't freak out, Destiny, we'll help you get free. Just stay calm and try to help us by pulling yourself out with your front claws. Panicking will only make matters worse," Tiger instructed encouragingly.

Tiger jumped to Destiny's side and started to excavate the rocky soil around her in hopes to free her trapped pelt. Midnight dug a hole on the opposite side of the fence with the help of Cassidy and Angel. Meanwhile Shadow got behind her and pushed with all his might.

Between the loose dirt, shoving, and Destiny's own pulling she finally made it through. Tiger followed after her, and then Shadow, letting his belly fur brush the dusty ground.

Once everyone was clear of the fence, the Village Cats led the Moonshine Clan through a maze of more shelters, or as Angel called them, houses. After running a right good distance, the group came to some woods. The cats quickly zigzagged through the oak trees and up to a gushing river.

Shadow figured this was the exact same river he and Angel had eaten the reddish-gray trout at several days ago. However, it must be closer to the mountains because he didn't recognize this particular section of it. Looking around he also didn't see the beaver's tree-lined dam anywhere nearby. Just as Sandy had instructed, they were near the bend of the river. As the group of cats reached the rushing river current, Tonk came to a stop.

"This is where we depart," he stated, indicating he was ready to get rid of them.

"Thank you all for helping us! We couldn't have made it this far in our journey without your help," exclaimed Midnight, clearly not recognizing Tonk's intentions.

"Don't mention it. Just follow this river bed. It should lead you somewhere up to the mountain," Marcus advised.

"We'll do! Maybe we didn't get your clan in trouble with the Black Widow Gang," replied Tiger.

Shadow's head was spinning in circles, he had been so caught up in the dangers of their new journey to the mountains he had forgotten about the Village Cats. They were leaving to get back to their camp before the gang showed up. This meant Angel would be going, too!

What if I never see her again? he thought.

In his heart, Shadow knew most likely he wouldn't. His heart started to pound against his ribs as he listened to the she-cats say their farewells.

"Good-bye, Destiny and Cassidy. Good luck on your trip!" exclaimed Abigail.

"Thanks! We hope the gang will leave you alone," proclaimed Destiny.

"Hopefully they will; it's not the first time they have threatened us. Maybe we'll meet again someday," Lena agreed.

"You never know, but at least our paths crossed. We'll never forget you and your gracious hospitality," Cassidy declared.

Shadow knew he had to say something to Angel, but he had no idea where to start. He wanted to express his sincere thanks for all her clan had done and the friendship she had given him since their arrival.

"Angel, I—," he muttered in a choked voice.

"No, Shadow, don't thank me," she interrupted. "I am so glad we found you in those draining caves and brought your clan to our base. I have had a lot of fun over the past days and consider you to be one of my most treasured friends. I will always remember all the special talks we shared and will keep the memories in my heart forever. Who knows, maybe Lena's right. Perhaps our paths will meet again someday in the future."

"Hurry up, we don't want the gang to spot us coming back from here," Tonk grunted, eyeing Angel and Shadow before taking off toward the woods.

Without wasting any more precious time, Marcus followed the gray tom with Abigail and Lena close behind him. Angel took one last look at Shadow before following her friends.

"Good-bye, Shadow. Continue to follow the Creator's North Star. May it guide you and your friends to your new home," she whispered.

"Good-bye, Angel. I'll never forget you!" he exclaimed, as she bounded after the others. Then, when she was almost out of sight he silently added to himself, "I love you so much, Angel."

"Let's go," Tiger urged as he began trotting swiftly in the opposite direction the Village Cats had gone.

Destiny traveled beside him, staying close enough for their pelts to brush. Midnight and Cassidy followed them with young Daisy and Lily scampering behind their parents.

"We better catch up, Shadow," mumbled Milo sorrowfully.

Shadow fell in line with him and the others, but with every step his heart grew heavier. Milo said nothing more; however, Shadow was sure it was because he felt there was a need for some privacy.

Until today he didn't think he was in love with Angel. Now Shadow knew he was. Grief and sorrow poured through his soul as if he had just jumped head first into the gushing river. Every muscle in his body felt weak, and the huge lump in his throat seemed to be growing as big as a rock. Shadow desperately wanted to go back to her, but he knew he couldn't leave his friends.

Without thinking, Shadow stopped walking. Milo turned and found him gazing back toward the woods.

"What's wrong?" Milo asked, getting the attention of the others.

Everyone froze, and with sincere faces his friends gathered around trying to comfort him. Little did they know his feelings of helplessness had more to do with Angel than their circumstances. Although the clan needed a safe place to live, not having Angel in his life ruined everything.

"Why are all these bad things happening to us? Our life seemed to be getting better. Now we have to start over again. How much longer will we have to live like criminals," he burst out.

"I don't know, but we are a family and we'll get through this storm together. Like you have been saying, a rainbow will come, we just have to keep on believing and trusting the Creator," explained Milo.

Shadow gave his little friend a weak smile as he tried to put on a brave face. The youngster's kind words didn't help much, but he was right. The Creator would get them through it.

Chapter Fourteen

A mixture of wind and rain pounded the Moonshine Clan. They were still on the journey to the mountains, although they had come a long way so far. It had been raining all day and part of the day before. Travel had obviously been slow, not only due to the weather, but also because they were constantly getting weaker. It was hard to catch enough food during the short hunts. They had followed the winding river upstream, as it wound its way toward the towering mountaintops.

Shadow felt like the river; his feelings were gushing through him like the rough current. He seemed to always be thinking of Angel, everything he did reminded him of her. The miserable heartache he was experiencing was the most agonizing torture he had ever undergone. He never knew anything could be worse than losing his beloved woodland home, but this situation topped everything. Not ever seeing someone you love was more devastating than having to give up your home. A home could be replaced; however, those you care about couldn't.

Out of all the clan members, Shadow was the most tired due to his lack of sleep. Everyone had done their best to be supportive and encouraging, but despite their good intentions, nothing helped.

As Shadow trooped on behind his friends, he couldn't help but feel anger toward Angel's clan. Part of him thought if they hadn't pushed them to leave so quickly he might have been able to convince her to come with them. In his heart he knew she would never be happy without her friends. She was a village cat, not a forest cat.

"Umm, I think we have a problem, guys," proclaimed Tiger, interrupting Shadow's private thoughts.

Shadow looked up to see that Tiger was right; they had come to two separate forks in the river. Studying the area, Shadow tried to figure out which way would be the best direction.

Then Tiger added, "Which way should we go?"

"I say we go up the right side of the river. The other side of the stream appears to go on around the base of these mountains, while this river weaves itself on up to the top," Midnight advised.

Agreeing, everyone nodded, except Tiger, who was reluctant.

"Okay, so we have a route. Now how do we get across it?" questioned Cassidy.

"Well, I don't know about the rest of you, but I'm not a good swimmer! There has got to be a better way," exclaimed Destiny.

Shadow realized Destiny was right; the current was too rough for them to cross, especially with the kits. Trying to find another way, he spotted a better idea. Up around the corner, just where the river split in half, Shadow noticed a log was lying across the roaring water.

"We could use that fallen log over there to get to the other side," he suggested, flicking his long black tail toward it.

Mewing in approval, the group of eight made their way toward the fallen log. As everyone gathered near the water's edge Midnight and Tiger debated which of them should cross first. Surprisingly, young Milo spoke up.

"I'll go first," the youngster announced.

"You will not do such a thing! It's much too dangerous for such a young cat. I refuse to let you risk your life," exclaimed his father sharply.

"Wait a minute, Dad, just hear me out. I know how dangerous it is, but I'm a lot lighter than you and Tiger are. My idea is simple; I could test it out for everyone else. If I fall in, then you, Tiger, and Shadow can pull me out of the river," Milo respectfully countered back.

Midnight gave his son a long look, clearly thinking over the process thoroughly. Although the idea was dangerous it was the best they had. After careful thought, Midnight finally let out a sigh.

"Okay, Milo, you can go, but please be careful. This is a very serious task," he stated firmly.

"Yes, sweetheart, please be careful," Cassidy urged with concern in her eyes.

Moving forward, young Milo stepped out onto the almost rotten log. He steadied himself with his sand-colored tail. Slowly making his way across it, Milo sunk his claws into what little bark was still on the log. As Shadow watched his young friend balancing on the log, he suddenly felt the same prickle of uneasiness he had gotten so many times before. He shivered, knowing what this feeling usually meant.

Something bad is going to happen to us today, Shadow determined. *I always get this awkward feeling when things go wrong. The Creator is trying to give me a warning.* To his relief, Milo made it to the opposite side of the river.

"Good job, Son. Alright, girls, it's your turn to cross," Midnight commented with a proud smile.

"Come on, Daisy and Lily! Just take it slow and keep your balance by holding out your tails," Milo instructed his sisters.

Glancing at their parents once more, the two young she-cat sisters followed in their brother's paw steps. Sticking out their tails, they slowly walked across the fallen log holding on for dear life. As soon as they were safely on the grass, Cassidy and Destiny made their way across as well.

By now, the heavy rain seemed to be coming down even harder. In the distance, Shadow could hear the rumbles of booming thunder as the storm clouds made their way over the mountaintops and toward the village. The sky was almost completely black, which made it harder to see around them.

Seeing the fallen log was now vacant, the toms decided to go together since the storm was getting closer. The last thing they needed was to get struck by lightning.

"Why don't you go first, Tiger? Shadow and I will be right behind you," Midnight suggested.

"Are you sure?" Tiger asked.

"Yeah, the log seemed to hold Cassidy and Destiny pretty good, so hopefully it will hold the three of us. The rain is getting harder so it would probably be best for all of us to cross as quickly as we can," Midnight responded.

Tiger gave Midnight a brief nod before approaching the log. The orange tabby tom stepped forward, followed cautiously by Shadow and finally Midnight bringing up the end. Walking carefully, all three toms filed out onto the surface of the log. As Shadow placed his paws out on the log, he could tell how rough the river's current was. Between the river water and the downpour of rain, he had to carefully watch his every step and had to make sure his claws were planted firmly into its surface.

In front of him, Tiger's paws slipped on the surface of the log, making his body off balance. Shadow froze and signaled to Midnight to do the same. To his complete horror, he heard a loud cracking sound. He knew very well what the sound was; they didn't have long to get off of the rotten log. Tiger finally got to his paws while trying desperately to scramble to safety with Shadow and Midnight on his paw pads.

The others had figured out what was taking place, because they were shouting for the toms to hurry up. Despite all of their clawing, the log split in half, sending all three cats sprawling into the gushing river. As soon as he hit the water, Shadow's body was engulfed with the ice-cold wetness. The back of his head hit something hard at the bottom of the river; however, he was so idled he had no idea what happened.

Dizzy from the impact of the object, he fumbled wildly for anything to keep him above the water. Unfortunately, the strong current of the river kept shoving him, taking him downstream. Everything around Shadow was water; he couldn't even see any of the others at this point. It took most of his power and strength to keep himself afloat; however, deep down in his heart Shadow realized he couldn't keep fighting much longer. He felt his paws, not to mention his other body parts, going numb from the icy cold water.

Soon Shadow could no longer lift his head for air. He just did not have the strength to do so. Exhausted and fatigued, he stopped fighting. With his head pounding from the injury, Shadow felt his body slowly sink into the freezing darkness. He was so cold he couldn't think straight, but in his mind faces started to come to him. His first thought was Tiger and Midnight telling him to never stop fighting. Next, he saw Cassidy and Destiny encouraging him to believe. Then, Milo, Daisy, and Lily were saying they needed him. Finally, Shadow saw Angel.

"Don't give up, Shadow. Keep fighting no matter what. I'll always be with you," she said.

Shadow suddenly felt a sharp tugging on the back of his neck. The pulling made his head hurt worse, but he was so weak he didn't move. Somehow as if it were a miracle, his body was slowly rising to the surface of the water. Still cold and weak, Shadow felt his body touch the soft ground where he came to a stop.

Opening his eyes, he found Milo was staring at him. As he coughed up water and gasped for breath, he realized the drenched Milo was vigorously licking his own flank, trying to keep him from shivering.

"Thank goodness, you're alive, Shadow! I wasn't sure that I reached you in time. Looks like you hit your head at some point. It's bleeding some," Milo stated between licks.

"You saved me, Milo? Thanks!" Shadow muttered weakly.

"Let's just say we're even," he replied, grinning broadly.

Milo helped Shadow stand up, supporting him as he staggered to a nearby mountain laurel. Cassidy met them while the others were waiting inside.

"Are you both okay?" Cassidy anxiously wanted to know.

"I think so. Can you help me get Shadow inside the bush? He hit his head," Milo explained to his mother.

"Absolutely! I'm so proud of you for saving Shadow. It was very brave of you to react so quickly. Weren't you afraid?" Cassidy hinted.

"I honestly didn't have to think about being scared. All I could think about was reaching Shadow before it was too late. After I saw you, Daisy, and Lily helping Dad, I knew I could find Shadow," Milo replied.

"Well, I sure was scared. When Lily told me you dove head first into the river I feared for your life. I just had to have faith that everything would work out and both you and Shadow would make it out alive. Thank goodness the Creator was protecting the two of you," she continued.

Cassidy smiled at her son as the two of them helped Shadow walk into the safety of the bush. Once inside, Shadow spotted Tiger curled up on the left side of the bush, while Destiny worked hard to get him dry. Midnight was on the right side, with his daughters busy on his own fur. Cassidy helped Milo stop Shadow's bleeding head with some spiderwebs and gave him a few leaves of catnip plant for fever before joining Midnight, Daisy, and Lily.

Taking a bite of the catnip, Shadow instantly tasted the irresistible minty flavor. He recalled seeing the spiky, purple-flowered plant back in the forest. Whenever one of them had a cold or fever they would eat the plant to get better. Shadow noticed Cassidy had also given Midnight and Tiger some catnip. He figured she had found it and the spiderwebs somewhere nearby.

"Milo," Midnight began when he saw them coming, "I'm so glad you are okay. The girls were just telling me about your heroic rescue. Looks like you managed to save Shadow. I'm so proud of you, Son."

"Thanks," Milo mumbled shyly, clearly uncomfortable in the spotlight.

Shadow took his place among his friends, watching Milo do his best to dry his soaked fur. He was shivering violently, but he was thankful he was alive and wasn't more injured than he was. Inside his heart, Shadow felt warm and cozy. His friends really did care about him, and so did Angel!

"So what exactly happened? The last thing I remember Tiger had lost his balance on the log. I recall falling into the river, but I couldn't see what was taking place with you guys," he asked feebly.

"Well," answered Destiny, "Tiger was close enough to the bank that he was able to find grip on the tall green grass. This enabled me to catch him quickly and to help pull his body out of the water."

"Midnight's side of the log spun around before getting caught on a rock. The girls held the log while I drug him out. He was lucky," said Cassidy.

"Unfortunately, you went under the water making it harder for us to spot you. When we did, I immediately reacted. I didn't even have a chance to think of a plan. My instincts took over," Milo added with a look of affection.

"Milo was really fast! He ran all the way downstream and wasn't concerned about his own safety. We were hollering at him to wait for our help, but he was determined. I guess it was a good thing because I don't know if you would have made it without his quick reaction," proclaimed Daisy excitedly.

"Then he bravely jumped into the river and pulled you out by the scruff of your neck!" exclaimed Lily.

Shadow smiled, he had no idea how strong and brave Milo really was. He said nothing to his friend, but Shadow knew Milo understood how thankful and grateful he was by the look the young tom gave him. He had saved Milo's life a moon and a half ago at the rock path, and now Milo had saved his in the river.

Deep inside the soul of his heart, Shadow knew the Creator had taken care of him in the same way He had saved Milo on the rock path. He felt so thankful to be alive and knew Milo would always be his best friend. As he looked back over his terrifying experience, he realized something else important. Angel would always be with him in spirit, no matter what. In such a short time, she had filled a very special part in his heart.

Who knows, he considered, *maybe her friend Lena was right.* Perhaps one day they'd meet again. With a tired smile, he closed his eyes and fell into a much-needed sleep.

Chapter Fifteen

Stretching his muscles, Shadow let out a gigantic yawn. He and the rest of the Moonshine Clan had been staying at the mountain laurel bush to regain their health. Hopefully today they would be leaving, after eating some fresh kill to give them energy for the journey.

Shadow, who was still a bit weak and sore from his ordeal, agreed to stay with Milo, Daisy, and Lily at their makeshift camp. Tiger and Destiny had gone up the river, while Midnight went with Cassidy down the river to find food.

Personally, Shadow was anxious to continue on their journey; however, to his surprise, the experience in the river drained his strength considerably. Although his head injury was nearly healed and he had eaten the catnip consistently, Cassidy felt he needed to take it easy since he still carried a slight fever. This was why the other toms insisted he stay at the camp, and not to exhaust himself any more than he had to.

Little did either of them realize how tiresome it was to watch three mischievous kits, assuming they were the ones who were cat sitting. All three of them, especially Milo, took the "taking care of" business very seriously. The siblings didn't even allow him to sit up.

For Shadow, who was independent, this was very frustrating. Despite the annoyance, he had to admit it was also amusing. He was lying on the mossy bedding watching the kits act like grown cats. Shadow realized how much they had grown up over the past two and a half moons. He knew it wouldn't be long before the three of them were old enough to go out into the world. Outside of the makeshift camp, a noise brought Shadow out of his daydreaming. The kits froze as they too heard the sound of breaking twigs.

In an instant, Shadow picked up the smell of a cat, one that didn't belong to any of the other clan members. The smell was so mixed up he couldn't decipher whether it was a tom or a she-cat, but the cat did carry a faintly familiar scent.

Shadow slowly made his way toward the opening, careful not to alert the intruder. He gently flicked his long black tail at the kits, telling them to stay back and to be silent. Daisy and Lily immediately obeyed, but hard-headed Milo remained opposite of where Shadow was standing. Shadow eyed him seriously, while Milo gave him a brave and determined look.

Knowing Milo was obviously not going to back down and follow orders, he let out a sigh while putting his concentration back on the intruder. He hoped this cat wasn't a part of the Black Widow Gang; however, this wouldn't be the first time the gang had tracked them down.

Deciding to take action before an attack took place Shadow dropped into a hunter's crouch and scented the air for the cat's exact location. He took a long, deep breath to calm his nerves, gave Milo a warning to not follow him, and quickly pounced down on his target.

Luckily, Shadow landed squarely on his opponent's shoulders, knocking it off balance. The two of them tossed and tumbled out of the mountain laurel bush and into the beaming sunlight. Milo and his sisters followed them, and watched with wide eyes at the fight.

The attacking cat was strong and powerful, but Shadow had achieved the element of surprise. He was able to pin the intruder down with his unsheathed claws. Weak with fatigue and gasping for breath, he expertly held the intruder flat on its back as he peered down into its face.

"Shadow, it's me, Angel!" she panted, as she too gasped for air.

Shadow was in so much shock, he nearly collapsed on top of her.

"What? It can't be!" he proclaimed, letting go of her body and backing away.

Realizing the intruder was Angel, all three kittens come up to greet her, explaining in great detail why they attacked her. Shadow didn't say anything; he still couldn't believe his eyes. Angel had come back!

This is the best day of my life, he decided. *Why did she come back? Was her clan attacked? How did she find us? Does she know how much I missed her? What will I do if she leaves again?*

Shadow had tons of questions for her, but he wasn't sure if he really wanted to know the answers to all of them. While he debated over his questions, Milo invited Angel inside the makeshift camp. Daisy and Lily continued to fill her in on all the adventures they had including Shadow's near drowning in the river. Exhausted, Shadow followed them inside and settled back down in the moss to rest.

"Are you okay? It sounds like you have been through a lot. Does your head still hurt?" Angel asked with a concerned voice.

"I'm fine, though I'm tired. My head injury is much better, but I still have a little fever. Thankfully, I was very blessed Milo was able to rescue me," Shadow responded.

"Wow, Milo, you were mighty brave to risk your own life for Shadow. I'm sure everyone is very proud of you," Angel praised the youngster.

"We sure are; he's definitely a hero. Milo, why don't you take your sisters to the river and get some water for Angel? I'm sure she is thirsty from her long journey. Just be careful and come straight back here," Shadow suggested.

Milo gave him the same look he had given him when Angel left: the look of understanding. With a smile, the youngster motioned for Daisy and Lily to follow him outside.

"Sure, Shadow!" he exclaimed leading his sisters out of the camp.

When they were alone, Shadow spoke up.

"So, why did you come back? Did the Black Widow Gang attack your base? Is anyone hurt?" he implied.

Angel looked away, as if she was uncomfortable answering his questions.

"No, the gang didn't hurt us, although they did look for you guys. I, well, I sort of chose to come back. You see, Shadow, I have always wanted to be a part of a clan like yours; a clan with no leaders or rules and one that is more like a family than anything else. Don't get me wrong, I'll always feel close to the Village Cats, but I think I would be happier in the forest," she announced.

Shadow couldn't believe Angel actually wanted to be a forest cat. She was even willing to give up her whole world to become one. Something didn't make sense with what she said.

"So you're telling me you would rather be a forest cat than live in the village. Seriously, Angel, don't tell me this was your only reason. I know you too well. No, there is something else, isn't there?" he inquired.

This time, she looked him straight in the eye.

"You're right, Shadow, there is something else. I was hoping you would take my first answer, because it's difficult and complicated to tell you everything. The real reason is because I want to be with you, Shadow. I didn't realize until we got back to the base how much I missed you. As soon as the gang left, I told Sandy where I was going, said good-bye to my friends, and tracked you down. I want to be with you and your clan," she declared.

Shadow was floored—just like he hoped she wanted to be with him as much as he did her. He wanted so bad to tell Angel he loved her, but decided to allow her the chance to get to know him better. After all, he didn't want to push Angel into a romantic relationship even he wasn't quite sure of.

"Thanks for confiding in me. I'm sorry you left your friends, but I'm so glad you have decided to live with us. Don't worry about joining the clan; I'll talk to everyone else. Just for the record, you would not believe how much I missed you!" he responded with a smile.

At this moment Milo, Daisy, and Lily came in dragging a curved leaf filled with water. As Angel drank, the three siblings told her more about the river incident, and how Milo bravely volunteered to go on the log first.

Even though they stretched Milo's lifesaving part, the smiling expression in Angel's eyes told Shadow she figured out it was a dangerous event.

It wasn't long before the familiar scents of the other clan members reached Shadow's nose. One by one the adult cats filed in and dropped off their fresh kill. Upon entering, the kits fell over themselves as they told Tiger, Destiny, and their parents of Angel's unexpected arrival. Noticing the others were baffled by her appearance, Shadow decided to tell them about her wish of belonging to the Moonshine Clan.

"What? Wait a minute, she wants to join our clan?" asked Tiger suspiciously.

"Yes, she does. Is there a problem?" Shadow countered calmly.

"No, of course not, but, Shadow, Tiger's right, why would she want to leave her friends and the Village Cats for us?" Midnight questioned.

Angel started to open her mouth to defend herself as usual; however, Shadow quickly cut her off. He felt since she stood up for him among her clan, it was his duty to do the same for his clan.

"She wants to live in the forest with us and stop living under the leadership of her clan and their numerous rules. Is that too hard to understand?" he implied.

At this statement, Tiger and Midnight looked at each other as if they weren't sure how to answer him. To Shadow's relief, Cassidy and Destiny spoke up in her defense.

"No, Shadow, it's not. We'll be glad to welcome her into our clan," declared Destiny, smiling at Angel.

"Absolutely! And Angel don't worry, you will make an excellent forest cat," added Cassidy, brushing her tail against her.

Angel smiled back at them, but Shadow sensed she still felt a bit uncomfortable. In his heart, he knew she probably wouldn't have come if he wasn't a part of the Moonshine Clan himself.

"Well, we had better eat and get started upstream. We have a whole lot of ground to cover by nightfall," Tiger announced.

It wasn't exactly a command, still everyone obeyed. Once they blessed the food, they devoured the fresh kill and made their way outside. As usual, Tiger and Midnight led, followed by the she-cats, and Shadow brought up the rear, with Milo and Angel on either side of him.

When the toms fell into the freezing cold river, they were sent downstream quite a long ways, meaning the cats now had to reach the same place where the river separated in two different directions. After they had traveled about halfway back, Angel softly spoke up.

"Umm, guys, why don't we just go straight up this mountain? I know it's steep, but it still seems like a better idea. We are a considerable distance from the village. I don't think the Black Widow Gang can find us way out here anyway," she suggested, coming to a stop.

Everyone stopped as well and turned to listen to what Angel had to say. Her idea did not sit well with Tiger.

"No, we are going to follow the river," Tiger responded firmly.

"But don't you think it would be quicker to go up here? After all, it's really a waste of time to travel back that far for nothing," she insisted.

Shadow winced. Angel had a good point, but arguing with Tiger was asking for trouble she didn't know she was getting into. Unfortunately Tiger was not going to let it go without proving his way was best.

"Following the river is not a waste of time or effort, and this is exactly what we're going to do," Tiger proclaimed sharply.

Deep down Shadow felt sure Tiger was no longer arguing about which way to go, but about his authority. Truth be told it didn't matter which way was best at this point; he just didn't like a newcomer telling him what to do.

"But—," Angel urged; however, Tiger abruptly interrupted her.

"No, for the last time we are following the river! If you want to go up the mountain, go alone. Just because you joined our clan doesn't mean you get to tell us what to do. Come on, guys, let's go," he declared, in an annoyed and enraged voice.

Angel folded down her ears, staring at Tiger with hurt in her eyes. This comment was too much for Shadow. Anger pulsed through him. He could normally control his feelings, but this was one time he wasn't going to let Tiger or Midnight run over him.

"I think Angel's right; we need to go up the mountain," he bravely countered.

"What? Don't be ridiculous," Midnight replied stunned.

"Oh, you do? Fine, you can go with her if you want to betray your clan. I don't even know why you stick up for her!" Tiger exclaimed.

"Tiger!" Destiny blurted out in shock.

With Tiger's outrageous comment, Shadow was so furious he almost wanted to rip his fur out. How dare he challenge him!

"I will go with her! At least I'm not as birdbrained as you are. You think you know everything, but you're wrong. Yes, I'm sticking up for her, whether you like it or not," he shot back.

Shadow took a few steps back and moved to where Angel was standing, separating himself from the others.

"Whatever. Midnight, are you coming?" Tiger questioned.

Midnight took one look at Shadow before he answered, "Sorry, Shadow, but I agree with Tiger." He moved toward Tiger and added, "Come on, Cassidy."

She and Destiny said nothing, but as they lowered their heads Shadow knew they would follow the toms. Watching his friends leave, his heart started to break. Despite his anger, he really loved them dearly. He didn't want to leave his family, but Shadow wasn't going to lose Angel again. Then all four she-cats turned and began to follow the toms when a voice piped up.

"Momma!" exclaimed Milo in shock, "I can't believe you agree with this."

Cassidy froze as the rest of the clan stopped to look back at the youngster.

"Shadow's been right before, so how do you know he's not now? He wouldn't be going with Angel unless he thought it was a good idea, too. You guys can do what you want, but I'm going with Shadow. There is nothing you can do or say to change my mind. I—I guess this is good-bye," Milo announced sternly.

"We're going, too!" shouted Daisy and Lily, darting back over to their brother's side.

At this point Cassidy spoke firmly, "I can't leave my kits, Midnight."

"I'm going as well, Tiger. Milo has a point, Shadow's plans usually turn out to be good ones," Destiny added.

Although neither Midnight nor Tiger wanted to go, the prospect of leaving Destiny, Cassidy, and the kits evidently was too much.

"Fine, let's go then," Tiger demanded with his ears down.

He and Midnight made their way to their leadership positions. To their surprise, Destiny and Cassidy held them back with their extended tails.

"You can go first, Shadow, we'll follow your lead," Destiny stated, while Cassidy nodded an approval.

Shadow could tell the toms didn't like this arrangement at all. Trying not to appear too confident or prideful, he signaled for Angel and the kittens to join him in front of the clan. Milo, Daisy, and Lily eagerly bounced along, excited to be leading the way for the first time. The she-cats went next, talking all the way while the toms followed closely behind in silence.

As the group struggled to claw their way up the steep mountainside, Shadow realized how thankful he was that his dear friend Milo spoke up. If the young tom hadn't done so, there wouldn't be a Moonshine Clan anymore. Shadow was also impressed by the courage Angel showed by not letting Tiger get the best of her. Both Milo and Angel had proved a remarkable amount of determination that no doubt the Creator had given them to stand up for what they believed in.

Glancing back at his fellow clan mates, Shadow promised himself he would try not to let any conflicting issues separate his friends. From now on, he would try his very best to keep the clan together no matter what.

Chapter Sixteen

With each step, the Moonshine Clan was getting closer to the top of the mountain. The long hike to the top had been a rough one. It had definitely tested the strengths and willpower of the Moonshine Clan as they made it to their destination.

Shadow had never anticipated how steep and rocky mountain climbing was until now. More than anything he hoped they would reach the summit soon. He also hoped the clan would find a suitable place to live at the top, so they could settle down and stop traveling. When Shadow looked up to see if the afternoon sun was above them, he noticed the tree line had stopped revealing the light blue sky.

"Umm, guys, I think we're almost at the top of the mountain," Shadow announced to his friends.

Everyone looked up to see what he was talking about. To Shadow's amusement he heard the three youngsters squeal with delight. The relief of almost being at the top must have given the group of cats a new surge of energy, because they reached the summit in a matter of moments.

Once the Moonshine Clan had made it to the top, all nine of them stopped to catch their breath and view their new surroundings. The Creator's magnificent scene before them was unbelievably gorgeous. Fields of evergreen fir trees lined a small dirt path leading to a large human shelter. The whole place was encircled by a wooden fence, obviously trying to keep out intruders. A smaller shelter was standing to the right of the massive one in the middle. From here, Shadow couldn't tell whether humans still lived there or not, but he was curious to find out.

"What do you think, guys? Should we go to have a look at the place?" Shadow questioned.

"Might as well. We have come this far. Let's be careful, though," advised Midnight.

"Yeah, I agree with both of you. This place might actually make a decent place to live," Tiger added thoughtfully.

At this point Shadow noticed Cassidy and Destiny giving the toms a hard look. To his surprise Tiger cleared his throat.

"Shadow," began Tiger, "I'm sorry for what I said the other day. My behavior was uncalled for. Angel, you were right and I was wrong. I just hope you both can forgive me for being so hardheaded and not listening to your suggestions."

"I'm sorry, too. If we hadn't come this way we wouldn't have found this place. Hopefully, the Creator has led us to a location where we can make ourselves a new home," proclaimed Midnight.

"Please forgive me, too. I shouldn't have jumped to tell anybody what to do. From now on I promise to do better. Thanks for letting me continue to stay with your clan," Angel apologized.

"I said some things I'm not proud of either. I should have controlled my feelings better," Shadow declared.

Now that the four of them had forgiven each other, the clan made their way toward the fence surrounding the evergreen fir tree farm. Shadow approached the wooden fence first. He noticed it was strangely different from the one they had gone under back in the village. This one was built with long wooden poles crisscrossed so they stood upright at an angle.

Without hesitating, Shadow quickly pushed himself beneath the lowest wooden pole with Angel close behind him. Knowing how to tackle fences, he easily got enough traction to go underneath it. Milo followed the two of them swiftly, with young Lily and Daisy hot on his paws. Next went their mother, Cassidy, and Destiny, who didn't get her fluffy white fur stuck this time around. Midnight and Tiger followed the she-cats briskly.

After the entire Moonshine Clan was safely under the fence, they slowly trotted down the small dirt path lined with evergreen fir trees. Shadow led the way, realizing how unkempt the trees were. It was obvious the humans hadn't been anywhere near this tree farm in quite a while, which in the cats' case was a good thing.

Scenting the air for dangers, Shadow picked up the strong scent of fresh kill. He did notice a vague smell of humans, but could tell their awful scent was fading away probably from the immense amount of rain. Chances were these particular humans had been gone for several moons.

Shadow felt sure the humans had abandoned this tree farm for good. As the clan advanced closer to the main yard, they approached it with complete vigilance. They all knew now from experience, someone or something might have already claimed this place as their own. Although the humans were gone, other animals could be living inside. None of them wanted to come in contact with anybody as vicious as the Black Widow Gang had been.

Looking around, Shadow tried to figure out which of the two human shelters they should investigate first. Choosing the smaller shelter, which appeared to be a barn, he decided to ask his friends' opinion.

"I think we should have a look inside this barn first. What do you guys think?" Shadow implied.

"Sounds like a pretty good idea to me. Don't you think so, Tiger?" Midnight responded as he glanced over at him.

"Yep, let's go," the orange tabby answered.

Taking the lead, Shadow proceeded to the barn with the rest of the clan behind him. The barn itself was a colorless, antique structure having some rotten boards along the sides. The door to the structure was slightly open just enough for a cat to pass through to the inside.

With one quick look at his friends, Shadow cautiously squeezed himself into the opening and inside the barn. While the others silently filed in after him, he allowed his dark green eyes time to adjust to the gloomy darkness.

After letting their eyes adapt, the nine cats started to explore and investigate. Shadow scented mice everywhere, so strongly it was almost overpowering.

From what Shadow was able to see, the barn was rather large and contained a platform about halfway up the wall. The whole place was covered with golden yellow hay, both strewn across the floor and stacked high in bales. On one side of the barn there were all sorts of wooden sticks attached to human objects. Shadow figured they must use them to move the hay. The opposite side held three individual places where the humans kept their animals. There was also a wooden container for the animal's water and food.

"Why don't we climb these stacks of hay bales and check out that wooden platform up there? I'm kind of curious to see what animals or objects might be hidden from our view," stated Tiger.

"Good idea," Midnight replied with a nod.

Then, as quick as a flash, the two toms jumped easily from one bale of hay to another until they reached the very top. Cassidy and Destiny followed closely with the three youngsters, Milo, Daisy, and Lily, bouncing behind them. Last went Shadow and Angel, making sure not to knock the bales down.

Like the rest of the barn, there appeared to be a lot of loose hay. In the corner Shadow spotted an empty nest of leaves, hay, and moss. Scenting the air he could tell it was an active squirrel nest. He briefly wondered where the squirrels were and made a mental note of the location so he could find them later for a meal.

Seeing there was nothing left to inspect, the Moonshine Clan decided to descend and go check out the main, two-level shelter—or as Angel called it, a house. Back outside in the sunshine, the group climbed up onto the wooden front porch. Beside the porch was a round, wooden box with water filled to the top. The water looked clear enough to drink, which was a good thing. If they were going to live here they wouldn't have to go so far for fresh water. This way the rain would continually replenish their supply.

Tiger shoved his shoulder repeatedly against the entrance to the place in hopes to get it open, but the entrance refused to budge at all. Luckily, Shadow spotted a window which had been broken at some point. If everyone was careful, they could easily jump through the opening and into the house.

"What about this window?" Shadow questioned.

Everybody except Angel stared at him as if he was speaking like a squirrel instead of a cat. Then it occurred to Shadow that they had no idea what a window or porch was. Angel had explained what houses and porches were on one of their many private walks back in the village.

"I'm talking about this see-through stuff. We can jump through the broken window," he announced, flicking his tail toward it.

Shadow's friends all nodded and meowed in agreement while motioning for him to go first. With one swift pounce, Shadow went through the hole in the window and into the house. Angel went next, followed by the three youngsters, the she-cats, and finally the toms.

The house wasn't nearly as dark as the barn had been. This was mostly due to the fact the uncovered windows were letting in a considerable amount of sunlight. It looked like the humans had just left their things where they were. In fact, the whole house still had weird-looking things placed in different sections, but now they were heavily caked in dirt.

Angel led the way through the bottom half of the house, explaining what the humans would normally do in each section. This completely amazed Shadow, who had no idea she knew so much about their unusual behavior. To his understanding, the humans would eat and sit on some of the objects on the bottom half of the house, before going up to the top level to sleep.

While Angel described all these things, Milo roamed around the humans' sitting area. Shadow watched him out of the corner of his eye, wondering how long it would be before Midnight saw him.

All of a sudden Shadow spotted Milo shaking his hind quarters and pouncing on top of a cloth-covered object standing high above the wooden ground. As the youngster swatted at an odd bird hanging near the top of the human shelter, he accidently slid off the cloth. Clawing madly, Milo landed with a loud banging noise.

Startled by the sound, Shadow jumped in fright. Turning around, he realized he wasn't the only one whose fur coat was standing straight up.

"What was that?" Tiger questioned in shock as he looked around to see the cause of the commotion.

"Get down, Milo! What in the world are you doing up there, Son?" Midnight ordered furiously.

"I'm sorry, Dad, I was only trying to catch this bird. It's really strange, he didn't even run away. I think something is wrong with him," Milo proclaimed.

"Well, if the bird is sick we don't want to eat it, so come on down," Midnight instructed firmly.

"And please be careful, dear," Cassidy added.

"He's not sick, he's already dead. I've seen humans do the same thing in the village. They like doing this to birds, deer, foxes, and other animals to show off their hunting skills to other humans. I'm pretty sure they eat the meat first, but instead of burying the remains, they hang it up," Angel informed them.

"Gross! Those humans are stranger than I thought," Tiger commented.

The rest of the clan nodded as Milo walked to the other end of the platform where he could jump down easier. With every step the youngster took, the object he was walking on made a sound.

"This thing is cool! Look at me," Milo exclaimed as he started to prance back and forth on the platform making the beautiful sound.

"Do you know what the humans call the thing Milo's playing on, Angel?" Destiny inquired with excitement.

"It's a music-making thing. They play it with their front paws and use it to entertain other humans. Sometimes they even have big parties where lots and lots of humans come to hear a human playing the music thing," Angel told her.

"Can we play on it too, Momma?" Lily asked her mother.

"Please let us, Momma, we'll be careful, we promise," Daisy continued.

"Okay, but let Milo get down first. I don't want all of you up there at one time," Cassidy agreed.

Letting out a groan, Milo reluctantly got down so Lily could jump up to the musical object. Banging on it happily for a short time, she too got down so Daisy could try out their new plaything. Grinning at the youngsters, Shadow stepped forward.

"Now it's my turn," he announced with a smile.

Daisy quickly got down as she and her siblings laughed at Shadow. The adults also giggled in amusement; however, Shadow didn't care, he was almost a kit himself. Jumping up to the music object, he skipped over the black and white things which made the music play. After a few moments he jumped to the wooden ground.

"Hey, I was pretty good at it," Shadow declared.

"How sweet, you were almost as good as Milo, Lily, and Daisy," Angel teased him playfully.

"Well, let's go check out the rest of the shelter. It's starting to get dark. Shadow can practice his so-called musical skills later," Tiger pointed out with a chuckle.

Laughing, the group continued exploring everything on the bottom. Then Angel led the nine cats up to the sleeping quarters on the upper level. They used the same wooden walkway the humans had made to the top. When they reached it, Angel again led the way around.

On their search, they came to the last section of the place. This one, like the others, had a window and a massive human sleeping thing in the center of the area. Since the sun was setting fast, it was quickly getting harder to see what was around them.

"Do you think it would be okay if we stayed here for the night? It's getting rather dark outside, and it would be a whole lot better to sleep here where it's safe," Cassidy asked in a concerned voice.

"I suppose we could. There doesn't seem to be any other animals living here at the moment so I think we would be okay," Midnight answered her.

"Great! I'm exhausted from traveling all day. It sure will be nice to sleep on something more comfortable than rocks!" exclaimed Destiny.

At that moment, Shadow heard Milo squeal with delight.

"Come here, guys! You won't believe what I just spotted. It's so amazing!" he shouted excitedly.

Milo's sisters bounded over immediately, as the adults gathered together to see what the young tom was yelling about. They all seated themselves side by side on a large wooden box positioned underneath the window.

What Shadow saw was glorious! Since they were high above the trees, he could actually see a great deal of the village below. The sun was setting in the opposite direction, which gave a wondrous effect. With the moon and stars starting to appear, it was almost like being out in the open.

From here, Shadow could see the river they had followed, as it wound its way toward the village. Even though the village was actually a right good size, up here it seemed to be diminutive. Shadow felt like he could fit it in his paw.

I wonder if I can see our forest home from here, Shadow contemplated. *It might not even be there anymore. We have been traveling for over two and a half moons. Surely, those humans have completely taken over by now.* Just then he saw what he was hoping for.

"Guys, look, there is our forest! Our home is right where the village stops. Do you see it?" he proclaimed happily.

"Well, what do you know," mumbled Midnight in disbelief.

Even Tiger smiled at the sight of their old home. Though the place was mostly the humans' shelters, there was still a tiny bit of the forest left.

"Is that really where you used to live?" Angel asked in surprise as she looked over at Shadow.

"Yes, it is," answered Shadow smiling.

"As much as I would love to sit here and chitchat about old times, I am very exhausted and hungry," declared Destiny as she descended off the wooden box.

"Come on, Midnight and Shadow, let's go back to the barn and kill some mice," Tiger suggested.

"Okay, Milo, why don't you come with us so you can practice," Midnight added.

All four toms headed down to the bottom level of the shelter. Meanwhile Destiny, Cassidy, Angel, and the girls jumped up to the giant human sleeping thing and made a place to sleep.

As Shadow trotted down the wooden walkway with Milo by his side, he thought about their new place. He was glad to finally have somewhere to rest without having to worry about trouble or dangerous animals attacking them in their sleep.

Jumping through the broken window, the four toms made their way toward the barn where earlier the scent of fresh mice was overwhelmingly strong. Shadow licked his jaws in anticipation of the delicious meal he was about to savor. Smiling, he looked upward at the pink and orange sky, noticing the stars were beginning to appear. Gazing at the Creator's beautiful scenery, he felt so thankful that the Creator led them to this place. Hopefully it would turn out to be a safe place to stay. Following Milo inside the barn, Shadow realized it didn't really matter if he had a home as long as he had the Creator and his beloved family by his side.

Chapter Seventeen

oderate heat radiated down from the clear blue sky. The usual pleasant, cool breeze had ceased since yesterday. This left no comfort in the Moonshine Clan's plans to organize their new home. Ever since they had arrived, the clan had been laboring day in and day out. They all strived for the security they hadn't had for moons. That was why they were not only making their new home comfortable, but also adding methods to warn them of intruders.

Shadow knew it wasn't going to be easy, nothing ever was; however, he had no way of knowing how hard it was. The balmy heat only added to the problem by tiring out the clan, which led to frustration and short-lived outbursts. These outbursts were mainly between Tiger and Midnight, but were quickly forgiven. Thankfully they had the wooden, water-filled box to quench their thirst. Otherwise they would have to walk a right good ways to the creek behind the house.

Right now, the toms were gathering moss for their sleeping bed. Meanwhile, the she-cats arranged the moss into better bedding. Shadow and Milo decided to check behind the barn for more moss. Midnight and Tiger headed down the dirt path and toward the evergreen fir trees.

Unfortunately, the woods behind the barn yielded nothing, forcing the two friends to look elsewhere. They doubled back and headed for the field behind the house. As they did so, Shadow saw Angel coming across the grass from the porch.

"Hey, wait up! Can we go with you guys?" she hollered at them.

"I thought you were helping Cassidy and Destiny fix the sleeping quarters," Shadow declared, a bit perplexed.

"Well, we were, but Cassidy asked me and the little ones to go find the two of you. She's pretty sure we have plenty of moss, so she proposed we catch some fresh kill," she proclaimed.

Until now, Shadow hadn't noticed Daisy and Lily were with Angel. At first he thought this was odd, but he shrugged it off, figuring Cassidy had probably grown tired of dealing with her daughters. Knowing them, they, like their brother, had gotten bored with nothing else to do.

"Okay, we will go hunting then," Shadow agreed as he led the way toward the back field.

Soon, all five cats were among the tall evergreen fir trees. To Shadow's curiosity, Angel didn't speak a word to anyone. He looked into her eyes only to find excitement. Her whiskers were twitching, as if she was also holding something back. Apparently she couldn't keep it to herself any longer.

"Milo, you know how to hunt, right?" she burst out.

Milo stopped walking to look at her.

"Yeah, Shadow and Dad taught me how to hunt. Why?" he questioned, completely confused.

Shadow was confused, too; Angel already knew the answer to the question. He had told her himself.

"Maybe you should teach your sisters what to do. Your momma told me she has been showing them the fundamentals of hunting, but they haven't actually killed anything yet. We are pretty safe here, plus Shadow and I will be close by if you need help," she answered shyly.

Milo looked from Angel to Shadow and back again. Shadow could tell he was baffled by Angel's strange behavior.

"Look, Angel, I've never hunted without supervision before, but I think I can handle teaching them to hunt. You don't have to pretend, though. I know perfectly well you want to be alone with Shadow. All you had to do was say so," he declared with amusement. Then he added, "Well, guys, the lovebirds wish to be alone."

"Ooooh!" exclaimed the sisters in unison.

Shadow could tell Angel was embarrassed, and he couldn't blame her. He was embarrassed, too. When the three siblings were out of sight and earshot, he cleared his throat.

"So, what was so important you had to go through that torture to say?" he implied with a grin.

"Actually the girls really do need practice. Cassidy was just telling me how nervous they are when she takes them hunting. They couldn't even manage to pounce on their prey. Perhaps they will do better with Milo. He's competition," Angel explained.

"Come on, Angel, I'm not crazy, that's not the only reason you sent them hunting, is it?" Shadow prompted.

"Okay, okay, please promise me you won't tell a soul what I'm fixing to say. I wasn't supposed to share this secret yet," she pleaded.

"Don't worry, I won't say a word. Are you sure you want to tell me and break your promise?" he hinted.

"I didn't exactly promise to keep the secret from you, only Tiger. Daisy and Lily were starting to get bored this morning so Cassidy finally gave in and let them go play a chasing game. While they were chasing each other up and down the wooden walkway, Destiny told us a secret. Destiny is going to have Tiger's kits!" she announced bouncing with excitement.

"Really? Wow, I didn't see this coming. I never thought I would see the day when Tiger had kittens of his own. Wait a minute, Destiny hasn't told him?" Shadow questioned.

"No, not yet, Destiny said she wasn't sure how he would take it. She wanted to have our opinion on how to tell him without putting him through shock. I told her I didn't know anything, so I volunteered to occupy the girls outside. They needed some time to talk without the two of them squealing," she replied.

"Tiger is definitely going to be surprised!" Shadow exclaimed.

As the two of them talked about the news of kittens, Shadow thought he heard talking. After scenting the air he detected the scents of Milo, Daisy, and Lily. Notifying Angel with his tail they changed subjects while waiting for the youngsters to return. It wasn't long before the three siblings showed back up.

"Are you finished talking?" Milo asked.

"Hope we didn't interrupt your romantic conversation," declared Lily laughing.

"We have caught enough for the whole clan. It was so much fun. For a while there I didn't think we were going to kill those mice, but Lily and I were determined not to let Milo get the best of us," announced Daisy.

"Yeah, Milo challenged us to a mouse face-off. The goal of the game was to see who could kill the most mice. The worst part of killing them was looking at those pitiful, beady eyes. After several mess-ups, Daisy and I teamed up. Between the two of us we were able to tackle and kill our first mouse. Daisy killed the first one and I got the second. It didn't take long for us to outnumber Milo's pile," Lily proclaimed.

"Then he had the nerve to tell us we couldn't help each other. It was against the rules he had just made up," Daisy added in an annoyed voice.

By this time Milo was grinning, "Well, at least you both got over your fears. Wait until Mom and Dad hear about the hunt. Anyway, did you say you were finished talking?"

"Yes, we have finished talking," Shadow answered, smiling at Angel.

Quickly, the group went to where the fresh kill was. They picked up the meat and set off back to the farmhouse. Shadow was both surprised and pleased the kits had caught so much.

Making their way back, the five cats took the food around to the front. When they rounded the corner, Shadow saw Cassidy and Midnight sitting calmly near the entrance. As they approached, he could tell by the look on Midnight's face he too knew the secret.

"Guess what, Mom and Dad? I helped Lily and Daisy get over their fears of hunting. I came up with this brilliant idea and challenged them to a mouse face-off," Milo announced joyfully.

"He didn't stand a chance after we figured out how to work together. It was easy once we got over staring at those beady eyes," Lily told her parents.

"Those beady eyes will get to you if you let them, but we weren't going to let Milo beat us at his own game. How does it feel to be beaten by two girls? Didn't think you would lose, did you?" Daisy continued directing the last part at Milo.

"I felt bad for you so I sort of let you guys win," Milo hinted sheepishly.

"Ha! I don't think so. You will just have to admit you were defeated by girls!" Lily responded triumphantly.

"We are so proud of both of you! Congratulations on your first kill!" Cassidy exclaimed as she gave them a lick of affection on their foreheads.

"Yes, you have accomplished quite a task. Getting over the fear of those beady eyes is a big achievement. You did a good job motivating your sisters, Milo. We are very pleased with your loving patience and hunting skills," Midnight complemented his kits with pride in his yellow eyes.

"Why don't you kits go play in the barn before we eat? Leave the mice with us. We need to talk privately with Shadow and Angel," Cassidy suggested.

Nodding in obedience, Milo, Daisy, and Lily piled the mice together and headed for the barn. Once the three kits were out of earshot, Cassidy spoke.

"The toms just got back. I came out here with Midnight so Destiny and Tiger could be alone. Angel, I know we had a promise, but only not to tell Tiger. I hope you understand," she proclaimed.

"Oh, I understand completely. I couldn't stand it either; I told Shadow while we were out hunting. Don't worry, though. The kits know nothing about the secret. The three of them hunted while Shadow and I talked about the news," Angel replied.

"It's pretty strange thinking of Tiger as a father, isn't it?" Shadow asked.

"You can say that again. I nearly passed out, I was still getting used to them not arguing. Boy, do I feel sorry for him! Don't take this the wrong way, I love my kits dearly. However, they are hard to raise, especially toms," Midnight stated.

As if their words had summoned him, Tiger jumped through the broken window. His head was down and his ears were folded back. In fact the orange tabby tom was in so much shock he didn't seem to know how to act. When he reached the others, Tiger paused briefly.

"She wants to see you, Cassidy," he muttered as he began to walk blindly down the tree-lined dirt path.

While watching the orange tabby walk away Cassidy gave Midnight a nudge and motioned toward Tiger.

"You should go with him, Midnight. Maybe you can give him some encouragement or at least show your support," she recommended with concern.

Midnight gave her a nod of understanding before leaving the porch and trotting after Tiger. Shadow briefly debated whether he should go, too; however, he decided Midnight needed to be alone with him since he knew how he felt finding out he was going to be a dad for the first time. Hopefully the Creator would help Midnight say the right words. Once the two toms were gone, Cassidy quickly made her way inside the house. At this point Angel looked at Shadow.

"I guess we need to take the fresh kill inside. Should we go get the kits first?" Angel whispered to Shadow.

"Let's take part of this meat inside before we go get them," Shadow answered.

Taking the lead, Shadow picked up several mice by their tails and jumped through the broken window. Landing in the house, he and Angel carried the fresh kill to the human eating area. They then laid the mice in a pile.

"Maybe we should go check on Destiny while we are here. You know, just in case she or Cassidy needs something. That way we will know whether we should bring the kits to the sleeping quarters or keep them occupied," Angel hinted.

"Good idea," Shadow replied.

Heading up the wooden walkway to the top, Shadow and Angel made their way to the sleeping quarters. As they were about to push their way in the entrance, Shadow heard a concerned voice. He paused, not knowing if they needed to interrupt the two she-cats. Behind him, Angel did the same, as Destiny's voice spoke out.

"I don't know, Cassidy. Tiger was pretty shaken up. After I told him about us having kittens, I thought he was going to faint. I have never seen him act so nervous. Do you think he will be okay?" she was saying.

"It will take some time for him to get used to becoming a father, but eventually he'll overcome it and be supportive. Midnight acted the same way when I told him about our first litter. Hopefully Tiger will feel better about the news after he and Midnight finish talking," Cassidy answered.

The two she-cats continued to talk. Cautiously, Shadow and Angel eased their way back down the wooden walkway trying to be quiet. Once on the bottom level, Shadow stopped to look at her.

"I don't know about you, but I sort of felt uncomfortable about interrupting their private conversation," he mentioned.

"Me, too. I think they need more time alone. We'll go get Milo, Daisy, and Lily. They can help bring the remaining meat into the house. Perhaps we can play a game or something until Midnight comes back with Tiger. Then we can all eat," Angel urged.

Leaving the house, the two of them trotted over to the barn. They had barely made it inside when Milo nearly knocked them down.

"Watch out, guys, coming through! Daisy and Lily are chasing me!" Milo shouted as he pelted past them.

Before Shadow could say a word the two sisters came squealing into view as they chased their brother. Fortunately Angel took over at this point by standing in front of the girls and holding out her tail in an effort to stop them. Seeing Angel in their way, they skidded to a halt in front of her.

"Come help me and Shadow take the food into the house," Angel instructed them.

Angel didn't have to tell the girls twice. Both sisters stopped chasing Milo and headed out of the barn toward the house. Apparently hearing Angel's comment, Milo quickly caught up with them and hit Lily with his tail as he ran in front.

"Bet you can't catch me!" he hollered.

As the three youngsters chased each other yet again, Angel and Shadow shook their heads. Those kits could always make anything a game. After they each picked up a mouthful of mice tails, they jumped into the house and placed the mice on the pile Shadow and Angel had already made.

While the three kits continued to play their chasing game, Shadow and Angel watched in amusement. The three of them ran in circles around the human sitting thing and then through the eating area. When Milo came back into the sitting area, he jumped up onto the music thing and ran across it making music as he went. Of course his sisters followed his lead, pounding the black and white platform with their paw pads. Leaping down they took off yet again.

Trying to avoid being knocked over Shadow and Angel settled on a human sitting thing. This one was wooden and rocked when you jumped on it. Sitting side by side the two of them watched the kittens from their perch. Shaking his head, Shadow laughed at them. He could hardly believe the events of the day. *Tiger and Destiny are going to have kittens soon. Milo, Daisy, and Lily caught fresh kill all by themselves. Plus, to top it all off, they had a new home. Wow, our Creator is really making life better!*

Chapter Eighteen

Nothing in the entire world could make Shadow leave the tree farm. He didn't know what he enjoyed more: the fresh air, the beautiful view, or the comfort of the headquarters. Today was rainy, but he didn't care. The whole clan stayed dry inside the spacious house.

Tiger and Midnight discussed and tried out new hunting techniques. Right now, the two toms were tussling madly with each other; their claws remained sheathed for safety. Cassidy and Destiny were debating on several names for her and Tiger's kittens. They had decided to pick out at least three names; however, so far the names all sounded girlish.

Lily and Daisy wanted to play a hiding game, so Milo went to ask Shadow and Angel if they wanted to play. They were sitting on a hard human sitting thing positioned in front of the musical object. Sitting on his hind legs, Shadow tapped the black and white things with his paws while Angel played with the ones on her end. Together, they played the musical object beautifully as soft music flowed out of it.

"That sounded pretty good. You guys are really talented when you bang on it at the same time. I know you want to keep playing, but Lily and Daisy wanted me to ask you something. Do you guys want to play a hiding game with us?" Milo implied.

"Sure, why not? Angel and I can practice playing this thing later," Shadow responded.

"Yeah, we would love to play with you. It's been awhile since I last played the hiding game," Angel added with a smile.

"Great! I can't wait to get started," Daisy proclaimed in excitement as she and Lily joined them.

"Me, either. I have been hoping to play the hiding game for quite a while. Every time we get a chance, something comes up. Today will be good, though. It's raining, so we have plenty of time," Lily continued.

"To refresh everyone's memory the object of the game is for one of us to count to ten while the rest find a place to hide. Then the one who counts must find everyone else," Milo declared.

"Why don't you count first, Milo? Daisy and I go first all of the time," Lily suggested eagerly.

"Okay, I don't mind," Milo agreed as he trotted up the wooden walkway to the upper level and closed his eyes.

As the young tom started his long dramatic count to ten, everyone took off in different directions desperately looking a place to hide. Daisy immediately headed under the nearest sitting thing. Lily followed her, but she expertly climbed up the window cloth instead. Shadow ran into the eating area with Angel, skidding around like they were on ice.

He looked around wildly for a good hiding place and spotted the flush wood above the human's food keepers. Knowing Milo should be headed down by now, Shadow pounced onto the counter and then onto the shelf. Angel followed close behind him, her eyes full of excitement.

The two of them then positioned themselves in a comfortable spot. Scarcely a minute went by before Milo's sandy coat ran into the sitting area. From where they were hidden, Shadow and Angel watched his every move, softly chuckling as Milo peeped around the corner at the sitting area.

At that very moment, Lily's weight gave way, sending her screeching and sprawling to the ground. Luckily, she didn't get hurt as she landed on her paws, but to her complete dismay Milo couldn't help but spot her.

"Hello, Lily, nice of you to drop by!" he exclaimed laughing.

"Hello, Milo, and for your information, I knew perfectly well what I was doing," she answered with composure.

"Yeah, right. I'll believe you when mice grow wings and fly!" Milo commented with a smile.

Shadow could hardly stop himself from laughing at the two of them. It was so funny watching Lily act as if she had planned to reveal herself so easily to her brother. Clearly she wasn't willing to give him the satisfaction of finding her.

"So one cat found and three to go. Well, I guess you wouldn't like telling me where Daisy, Angel, and Shadow are hidden?" Milo kidded as he began to circle every human thing in the area.

"Absolutely not! I'm not a tattletale," Lily replied sharply. Then she added in a matter-of-fact way, "Oh, and don't you even think about scenting them out, because it's not fair."

Milo said nothing, while rolling his eyes in disgust, despising being told what to do. He rounded the largest human sitting thing and stopped dead in his tracks. Shadow saw a grin creep onto his face as he stared down at the sand-colored tail tip before him. Ever so softly, the youngster bent down and nipped his sister's tail, sending her bolting out the opposite side yowling in protest.

"Ouch! Why did you have to do that?" she screamed.

"Hi, Daisy. Boy, I'm good at hunting!" Milo remarked, grinning broadly.

"Yeah, I guess so, but you didn't have to bite me so hard," she declared, licking her tail gingerly.

"Come on, I didn't hurt you too bad," Milo countered.

Shadow could tell each of the kits took after their parents. Lily was a lot like her dad, proud and determined, while Daisy was more like her mother, agreeable and quiet. Milo, on the other paw, came from a different universe.

"All right, Shadow is more skilled and clever than you two. Plus, he won't reveal himself so easily. If I was Shadow where would I hide?" Milo questioned himself.

"What about Angel? Don't forget about her," Lily reminded him.

"Oh, yeah, well, let's look for Shadow first. Then we will go look for her," Milo decided as he continued his search.

"To answer your question, Shadow would probably go somewhere dark, since his coat is black," Daisy suggested.

Shadow had to give it to them; they knew him pretty well. He found himself thoroughly enjoying the entertainment of the three youngsters searching the eating area. This was especially intriguing because none of them ever looked up. Secretly, he felt positive they would never find him or Angel.

Angel, who had also been laughing, could hardly control herself either. Suddenly, Shadow noticed a flicker of mischief dance in her lime-green eyes. Before he knew what was happening, she turned over and kicked him playfully with her back legs. Between her powerful kick and his surprise, Shadow let out a shocked yowl. Although it wasn't really loud, it was enough to capture Milo's attention.

"Greetings, Shadow. Thanks for letting me know where you were concealed!" he exclaimed excitedly.

"Hey, that's not fair!" Shadow demanded, acting like he was a little mad.

With a swift movement, he shoved Angel back. Using his hind paws, he managed to knock her off balance.

"Shadow, how dare you!" she responded.

"Angel, you're up there, too?" Milo inquired from down below.

"Wow, I can't believe our luck. We found both of them at the same time," Lily declared in awe.

Despite Milo's question, no one needed to answer it. Seeing there was no longer any reason to continue to hide, Shadow jumped down onto the counter and then to the ground. Angel followed in hot pursuit, keen on tackling him.

She quickly caught up with Shadow and easily brought him down onto his back. Shadow struggled beneath her strong grasp, pretending to fight back.

"Please don't hurt me," he begged, laughing.

"Oh, I'm going to get you good," Angel announced as she put all of her weight upon him.

"Okay, I have found all of you," stated Milo.

Shadow acted as if he didn't hear the youngster, though he did stop fighting Angel. When Angel stopped focusing on him, he turned over on top of her. This time she couldn't avoid his powerful grip.

"Who's in trouble now?" he asked in amusement.

"I give in, I surrender," she replied, gazing deeply into his green eyes.

Being caught by her enchanting gaze, Shadow slowly let go of her. He was awkwardly conscious of the kits' watchful eyes.

"Was it really necessary for the two of you to tackle one another?" Milo questioned, cocking his head to one side in curiosity.

Angel and Shadow exchanged a look of embarrassment. Suddenly Shadow got an idea. Winking at Angel, he grinned at Milo.

"Of course it was," Shadow answered.

Then with Angel's help he jumped toward the kits, who squealed with pleasure as they scurried out of reach. The cats quickly forgot about the hunting game, being too occupied with the chasing one.

Eventually, the five of them had to stop due to fatigue, and they resumed a less exhilarating pastime. While they rested, Shadow noticed that the rain seemed to be getting harder outside. At this particular time he had an abrupt tingle go down his spine. Knowing the Creator normally gave him this feeling of danger, he scented the air. Sure enough, he smelled what he most feared: strange cats.

Shadow swiftly flicked his ears, signaling to the others to remain silent. He then led the way into the sitting area and under the human seat where Daisy had been hiding earlier. There was no time to warn the rest of the Moonshine Clan, so Shadow had to defend the house. Careful not to make a sound, he ducked into the dark space with the three youngsters and Angel behind him. Once they were all safely hidden beneath the seat, Milo quietly spoke.

"What are we going to do? Do you think those cats are members of the gang?" he questioned.

"I don't know if they are the Black Widow Gang or not, Milo. If they come in the house, I want you kits to go get Tiger and your dad. I'll deal with the intruders, and Angel can make sure you kits stay safe," Shadow responded.

Milo opened his mouth to say something when they heard the clanging of the small, round human objects that Angel said humans put food in. They had placed them on the floor beneath the broken window to alert them. Shadow didn't have to repeat his command, because as quickly as lightning, the three kittens took off to the sleeping quarters.

Angel followed them almost as quickly but stopped at the base of the wooden walkway just in case Shadow needed her assistance. Meanwhile, Shadow came out from under the sitting thing and faced the intruders with his back arched, claws extended, and teeth ready to fight whatever danger threw at him.

"Stay back and no one will get hurt!" Shadow addressed the intruders as he let out an agitated hiss.

"Hold on a minute. Don't attack us. We mean no harm! We're a part of the Village Cats, remember?" urged the dark gray tom as he struggled to get free from the human objects now strewn all over the floor.

"Tonk?" Angel asked in a completely baffled voice.

Shadow was totally flabbergasted; he had never expected to see Tonk or Marcus, who was with him, so soon. After hearing the noise, Tiger and Midnight rushed down the wooden walkway, closely followed by the she-cats and the kittens. They all froze when they recognized who their visitors were.

"Whoever thought of this was smart; it lets you know when someone's coming. Looks like you found a place to stay. Luckily we were able to track your scents most of the way before they were destroyed by the rain," Marcus declared, shaking his pelt free of rain water and sidestepping some of the objects.

"What are you doing here?" Angel asked point blank.

"Well, we have been traveling nonstop. Is it possible we can get something to eat?" Tonk replied, clearly not as impressed as Marcus was about the objects on the floor.

"Sure you can. Please make yourselves comfortable, Midnight and Tiger will be glad to get you some food," Cassidy proclaimed as she and Destiny led the way into the human sitting quarters.

Midnight and Tiger immediately went outside to the barn to kill a few mice. Meanwhile the two guests found places to rest among the gathered Moonshine Clan. Seeing they were occupied with licking their pelts dry, Angel pulled Shadow to the side so they could talk in private.

"Something is wrong, Shadow. They wouldn't come here just to visit, and Lena and Abigail aren't with them," she whispered.

"Are you sure you're not just overreacting?" he questioned quietly.

"I'm sure. Tonk was not happy when I left, and I doubt he would come to see me knowing I refused to remain there with him. You can tell he is annoyed by his sour attitude. He had to be sent by Sandy. It just doesn't add up," she responded softly.

Shadow said nothing more. He not only trusted Angel's words but also knew his own uneasiness. Besides, he now knew another one of Angel's secrets: Tonk did not want her to leave the Village Cats. This only meant Tonk probably despised him even more since Angel had joined the Moonshine Clan. Tonk was a lot like Tiger had been in the past, signifying one thing: Don't get in his way. Truthfully, Shadow didn't particularly like him either.

When Tiger and Midnight returned, they gave Tonk and Marcus the four mice they had killed and settled down to lick their drenched fur coats.

"Thanks for going out in the messy weather to feed us," Marcus commented before taking a bite of his mouse.

"You're welcome," Midnight replied between licks as he exchanged a questioning look with Tiger.

From his expression, Shadow figured the two toms had discussed why Tonk and Marcus had come. He wondered if they were concerned about this odd change of events. As everyone gathered around the guests, Shadow watched them devour the fresh kill as if they had traveled without much food. After eating, they began to explain why they had come.

"Our food is getting scarce and our cats are becoming weaker by the day. The Black Widow Gang told us we can no longer eat anywhere they call theirs. Unfortunately, they think they own everything in the village. Sandy decided to take back what has always been rightfully ours. Before we knew it, things went from bad to worse. We found out the gang killed three she-cats and left them for us to find later. Luckily, it wasn't Abigail or Lena, but one of the she-cats was expecting kittens soon," Tonk announced gruffly.

"Sandy and Comet sent us here to warn you about the Black Widow Gang. Their leader, Bombay, has made it quite clear he is going to hunt your clan down and kill all of you. He said he would be back to teach our clan a lesson and then plans on tracking you down. Considering Tonk and I were able to find your new home, it's likely they will be able to figure out where you guys are living also," Marcus added in a sympathetic tone.

For a long time no one spoke a word. Finally, Tiger broke the silence.

"Thanks for coming this far to let us know what was going on. I personally don't know what to do. The last thing we need is them finding our new home. So much for all the protections we put in place," Tiger muttered sourly.

"What if we—," Milo started as his father interrupted him.

"Milo, this is a very serious situation so it's probably best for you and your sisters to either sit quietly or go play," Midnight said sternly. Then he continued, "Perhaps we should go back to the village with you guys. Since they are so determined to attack us, it might actually be better to fight them in their own territory."

The three youngsters surprisingly were too interested in the conversation to go play. Following their dad's instructions, they all sat still and listened closely to what ways the adults were going to handle the upcoming trouble.

"We should probably go. At least we will have a better chance of survival with another clan. They will come after us anyway," proclaimed Destiny as Tiger nodded in approval.

"Yes, I agree it would be smarter to join with the Village Cats to stand against them. I don't like the idea of having to fight, but it looks like there isn't any other solution," Cassidy added.

Now everyone turned their attention to Shadow and Angel, the last remaining clan members. Shadow noticed Angel was looking at him with hurt and confusion. He could tell she wanted to go but wasn't quite sure if it was a good idea. She was looking for support and knowledge, like she had grown used to doing. Shadow felt like the Creator was leading him to the only logical answer, although he still wanted Angel to be the one to make the final decision.

"The gang is cruel, especially if they are willing to kill for what they want. Clearly they aren't willing to settle this in a respectful manner, so I suppose we will have to fight them. There is a huge possibility we'll lose this battle and have to retreat, but this way they won't find our new home. I'll make my decision based on whether or not Angel goes," he responded, giving her a supportive look.

Relief flooded into Angel's lime-green eyes.

"I think we need to go. There have been enough innocent lives killed or tortured by those evil cats. Battling the gang in their territory will be much better than waiting for an attack up here," she stated.

"Okay, that means we'll go then," Shadow continued.

As the adult cats started making plans on when to leave and which way was the quickest route to take with the kits and Destiny, Angel motioned with her tail for Shadow to follow her. She led him to the human eating area on the opposite side of the house. From here Shadow could see Milo and his sisters had finally given up on sitting still by resuming their chasing game.

"Thanks for letting me make my decision first, Shadow. It means a lot to me because Tonk and Marcus won't think I have betrayed the Village Cats," she stated.

"You're welcome. I noticed how they were looking at you. Hopefully everything will turn out okay and they won't defeat us," he replied.

"I don't know if we'll make it, but I'm going to hold on to what you said. You told me the Creator has a plan for us. Terrible storms have a rainbow and maybe this awful situation has one, too. We just have to trust the Creator with our lives," she declared, placing her forehead under his chin.

Chapter Nineteen

Going back to the village brought back the horrid memories of why they left. The Moonshine Clan, along with Marcus and Tonk, had been traveling for several days, hardly stopping to rest. They had decided to go straight down, hoping to reach the village sooner.

Shadow knew they didn't have long before the Black Widow Gang launched another attack, if they hadn't already. Even though he was exhausted from the rocky descent, the blazing fire in his heart gave him new strength. He had also noticed how tough the journey was on Destiny and the kits.

One by one, the group of cats finally reached their destination. Shadow recognized the bend in the river, the same bend where Angel had left him more than a moon ago. By the looks of things, the Village Cats had been forced to move out here by the river, most likely because of the endless supply of fresh trout.

There were cats all over the open field. Judging their miserable faces, Shadow could tell they were afraid of what was happening. They all looked up when they saw Marcus and Tonk leading the way into their makeshift base. It didn't take any time at all for Sandy and Comet to hear about the arrivals. Soon the two leaders were coming toward them in welcome.

"Hello, Tonk and Marcus. I see you had no trouble finding the Moonshine Clan. I'm actually surprised you made it back so quickly. I wasn't expecting to see you for at least three or four more days, and I didn't expect the Moonshine Clan. Angel, I am so happy to see you!" Sandy proclaimed.

Before anyone had a chance to explain why they had come, Angel's friends, Abigail and Lena, came out from the crowd of gathered cats.

"Angel, it's you, it's really you!" exclaimed Lena, as she and Abigail covered her in licks of affection.

"I didn't think we would see you again so soon," Abigail added.

"Me either. It seems good to be back with the clan, though I wish the circumstances were better," Angel responded.

"Yeah, unfortunately things aren't looking good at the moment," Abigail answered sorrowfully.

"Well, after we talk with Sandy I would love to tell you about the amazing place we're living at. I can't wait to catch you up on what my life has been like since I left," Angel stated excitedly.

"We are looking forward to hearing about it. I'm sure it has been quite an adventure," declared Lena, laughing.

Shadow smiled as he listened to Angel talk to her closest friends. Meanwhile Marcus explained to Sandy and Comet the reason that the Moonshine Clan had come with him and Tonk.

"So you decided to come down here so they won't discover your new home," Comet summed up.

"Yeah, we thought it might be wise to meet them on their own territory," Midnight responded.

"I agree that seems like the wisest decision. I know you must be tired and hungry from your exhausting trip. You are more than welcome to stay in the reeds beside the river with the rest of us. Comet, would you please take our guests there so they can rest? Meanwhile Lena and Abigail can fetch you some fresh fish. Once you have eaten, we can discuss further plans for the Black Widow Gang," Sandy commanded.

Everyone followed Comet to the edge of the river where the members of the Village Cats slept. The Moonshine Clan settled down among the reeds and, after thanking the Creator, ate the reddish-gray trout the she-cats brought to them. Shadow smiled as he listened to his friends comment on eating trout for the first time. Angel offered to teach them how to catch fish by using her fishing technique. Of course Milo wanted to learn first and questioned whether the creek behind the house had trout.

While they ate, they answered the Village Cats' many questions, much of which involved their new home. Soon after they finished eating, Tiger mentioned he smelled a foul scent and asked Shadow if he smelled it. Before Shadow could respond, Sandy and Comet arrived with concerned looks on their faces.

Shadow could tell, like he had done when he first met her, that she wasn't a typical leader. Sandy was a wise and passionate adviser to her fellow clan mates. He knew she was willing to do whatever it took to protect her clan at any cost, even if it meant laying down her own life. One thing was for sure: she was not going to allow the gang's leader, Bombay, the opportunity to take over.

"So, have you given much thought about how we should approach this problem? We obviously need to prepare for battle, but when do you suggest we execute an attack?" she asked in curiosity.

"Umm, I honestly don't know," Tiger answered.

"I suggest we wait for the Black Widow Gang to come to us," Shadow recommended.

"I see, and why should we wait?" Sandy implied.

"Well, whenever the gang decides to launch their attack, we will be ready for them. Not only will we be able to see our enemies more clearly, but fighting them here is easier than going into their territory. This way, they won't sneak up on us," he responded.

Sandy didn't speak at first. She seemed to be carefully considering his words, weighing the consequences.

After several moments of serious thought the tabby leader replied, "Okay, so what do you think about Shadow's idea, Angel?"

Angel looked surprised by her question, probably because her old leader had asked her opinion first versus Comet's.

"I think Shadow is right. It would be better if we achieved the element of surprise," she declared.

"Very well then. Comet, what's your opinion?" Sandy wanted to know.

"Seems like a logical plan to me," Comet agreed.

"That is what we'll do. We will start to prepare immediately. There is no telling when the Black Widow Gang will attack us, and we must be ready for anything. We will need a safe location for the kittens and their mothers to hide during the battle," Sandy proclaimed as she returned to her quarters.

As if his leader had sent out a command instead of a statement, Comet began to give out multiple orders of his own. The cats who received instructions promptly carried them out. Wanting to do their part, the Moonshine Clan offered to help out in any way needed. Grateful for any extra cats, Comet sent the clan out in pairs with the Village Cats.

Destiny was so tired from the long trip that she decided to stay behind with Daisy and Lily. However, Milo refused to remain with his sisters. Regretfully, Cassidy agreed to let him go with her and some of the Village Cats while Tiger and Midnight went with another group. Shadow ended up with Angel. Unfortunately, Tonk requested to go with the same group, probably because he wanted to keep an eye on Shadow.

Why in the world does Tonk feel he has to constantly watch me? Shadow pondered. *He has been sneaking around and keeping a check on where I am and what I have been doing ever since he and Marcus arrived at our home. What have I done to cause him to be suspicious?*

Shadow instantly realized the answer to his own question. Tonk wasn't necessarily watching him. The dark gray tom was keeping up with how many times he and Angel were alone. Angel was what Tonk wanted. If Tonk could convince Angel she missed her old home, she would move back to the village. She would be his girl again. Boy, was he clever!

By now, Shadow's group was searching for things to use to construct deadly traps. Everyone had split up into small groups, with Shadow and Angel working as a pair. This arrangement suited Shadow just fine. It gave him a chance to be with her without having the feeling of being watched. Taking advantage of this time, he decided Angel needed to know about his suspicions of Tonk.

"Angel," he declared uncomfortably, "there is something I need to talk to you about. It's kind of important."

Angel stopped what she was doing and sat down in front of him. She gracefully draped her long black tail neatly across her black and white paws and gave him her full attention.

"Okay, I'm listening," she replied.

Shadow took a deep breath, asked the Creator for guidance, and began to try to figure out the best words to describe how he felt. He didn't have a lot of experience expressing himself in this way.

"Look, you wanted me to get to know your friends. However, there is no way Tonk and I can do that. He doesn't trust me and does not care to have any kind of friendship. In fact I get the feeling he doesn't want me around, particularly when you and I are together. To be honest, his strange behavior has made me wonder if he could even be trustworthy," he stated firmly.

To his amazement, Angel only shook her head and smiled.

"Oh, Shadow, you're overreacting. Tonk has an odd way of doing things, but he and Marcus are friends. Once you get to know him, he'll warm up to you. I am glad you shared with me how you felt, though. I think the two of you are just jealous of each other. He told me the same thing last night. Toms can be so ridiculous sometimes!" she proclaimed, getting up and trotting through some ferns.

Shadow stared after her, speechless. He didn't know Tonk had talked to Angel previously. She acted as though it was no big deal and insinuated that they were jealous. Frankly there are times she-cats made no sense at all. It was like Angel was playing a game, to see which tom liked her most.

Maybe she had forgotten about Tonk's bossiness and decided to give him another chance. Whatever reasons she had, he was not going to allow Tonk to take over. If he wanted Angel, he would have to go through him first.

Sighing, Shadow decided to gather some sticks. While he did, he thought about what he could do to prove Angel was his. After what seemed a lifetime, Angel showed up with a few bunches of moss in her mouth. The two cats made their way back to the Village Cats' makeshift base. When they arrived, Shadow noticed the other patrols had come back as well. He dropped his sticks on the pile of other materials, just as Milo came up to him.

"Did you have a good hunt?" Shadow asked.

Milo and Cassidy had been on the hunting patrol, while Tiger and Midnight helped with securing the base.

"Yeah, the mice weren't so bad, but hunting with Mom was worse than with Dad. I had no idea what she was like. She was constantly reminding me to be careful and to stay close to her like I was still a kitten. No wonder Lily and Daisy had a hard time learning how to hunt. It's amazing Mom even gave them a chance," Milo replied grinning.

Out of the corner of his eye, Shadow watched Tonk arrogantly strut over to where Angel was seated. She was talking to her friends Lena and Abigail at the edge of the cattails and reeds. Milo followed his gaze with a questioning look on his face.

"Wonder why Tonk's going over there?" the young tom asked.

"I know what he's doing. He's trying to convince Angel to stay here," Shadow answered sharply.

"Oh, I see. He's trying to take her from you," Milo hinted, giving him a sideways look.

"Yeah, I guess you could say that," Shadow muttered awkwardly.

"You love Angel, don't you?" Milo questioned softly.

Shadow looked at Milo in surprise. He could hardly believe what his friend was saying. How did such a young cat know so much? Were his feelings for Angel so obvious a youngster could pick up on it?

"Yes, Milo, I love her. I can't let Tonk take her back because there is no way I can live without her in my life—even if it means I have to leave the clan. One day you'll understand how I feel," he proclaimed.

"I understand. Why don't you tell Tonk to leave your girl alone? I'll back you up, if things get nasty," Milo suggested.

Shadow had never thought about just telling Tonk to back off. Milo was right; he needed to stand up for what he believed in. With a brisk nod to Milo, he trotted over to where Tonk was talking with Angel, Lena, and Abigail. The rest of the Moonshine Clan were seated nearby, close enough to hear what was going on. Approaching, Shadow overheard Tonk asking Angel if she would eat with him.

"No, she doesn't want to eat with you," Shadow responded for her.

Angel said nothing; however, the look she gave him said she was not happy with him for answering in her place. Despite the fact she was upset she still kept quiet, clearly not wanting to embarrass him.

"Oh, yeah, and who asked for your opinion?" Tonk inquired sarcastically.

"It doesn't matter. Angel isn't interested in you, so from now on I want you to leave her alone," Shadow stated firmly.

"And who is going to make me? Are you going to, birdbrained fur ball?" Tonk shot back in a nasty tone of voice.

Obviously, the two toms had attracted a lot of attention as their discussion was beginning to get out of control. Lena opened her mouth to say something, but Shadow spoke before she could.

"Back off, Tonk, you don't know what you're getting into," Shadow declared defensively.

"Ha! I could take you down anytime, Pipsqueak. Angel is going to move back here with me. She is mine, not yours, and I better not catch you with her again," Tonk announced as he unsheathed his claws to prove his point.

Shadow was infuriated. Without thinking he let his own claws sink into the ground. His heart pounded as he tried to keep himself from slapping Tonk. Apparently Tonk was threatened by this because he attacked Shadow.

As Shadow tried to protect himself, the two toms rolled all over the ground with claws extended and teeth snapping. This fight was serious, and neither was taking it easy on the other. They were actually fighting as enemies.

Shadow felt Midnight and Tiger pulling him off Tonk, but Shadow refused to give in. Marcus and a few others dragged Tonk away; however, he wasn't going to give up either.

Somehow or another, Tonk managed to pin Shadow down as he prepared to claw his belly fur. Just when he was about to do so, Milo came out of nowhere and bit down on Tonk's long gray tail, yanking him off Shadow's body. Furious, Tonk turned on young Milo, but between Milo and Shadow, Tonk was knocked over. Now all three toms were tussling madly with each other. Suddenly, an enraged yowl sounded through the clearing, making every cat freeze and look up.

"I will not put up with this nonsense! The Black Widow Gang is going to attack us at any moment, and yet you are fighting here in camp. Who started the fight?" demanded Sandy angrily.

Getting up off the ground, Shadow looked at Angel. As their eyes met he could see she was hurt by what just happened. Milo and Tonk also stood to face Sandy.

"Tonk started it. He's out of control. Somebody needs to put him in his place. Maybe a nice long punishment will teach him not to go around making threats," Milo advised.

A deep growl rumbled in Tonk's throat at the kit's comment; however, Sandy silenced him with a flick of her tail.

"Silence!" she hissed.

At this point Midnight spoke, "Sandy, please forgive my son. He shouldn't have said anything about this, and shouldn't have been a part of it."

"Dad, you can't possibly think Shadow was the one who—," Milo blurted out.

"Milo, I don't want to hear any excuses. You are in just as much trouble as Shadow," Midnight cut in, giving his son a stern look to stop talking.

"Actually I think both toms were at fault. Neither of them would stop fighting when we were trying to pull them apart," Tiger told Sandy.

"I have to agree with you, Tiger. Tonk was fighting just as hard as Shadow," Marcus reported.

"Very well. Since Milo is still under your care, I will leave his punishment to you, Midnight. As for Shadow, since you are staying under my leadership you will get the same punishment as Tonk, which will be not eating tonight. I also think an apology would be appropriate," Sandy proclaimed, staring expectantly at the two toms.

Reluctantly, Shadow turned toward Tonk.

"I'm sorry," he muttered halfheartedly.

"Me, too," Tonk growled back through clenched teeth, though Shadow didn't think he was truly sorry.

At this point Midnight gave his son a look of dissatisfaction. It took Milo a few moments to figure out what his dad expected him to do, but he finally came to the conclusion he was supposed to apologize whether he wanted to or not.

"Sorry," Milo said awkwardly.

Satisfied, Sandy went back to her private quarters in the reeds as the other cats broke up into small groups ready to eat. As if Sandy had commanded it, everyone left the two toms alone. Nobody went near them, and it seemed clear they would have to sleep out in the open without the comfort or shelter of the reeds.

As Shadow searched the crowd for Angel, he spotted her with Lena and Abigail. As the three she-cats walked away, Shadow ran to catch up with them before they got to the fresh kill pile.

"Angel, I'm so sorry. I didn't mean for all this to happen," Shadow declared.

"Shadow, I don't think we should be talking right now," Angel responded as she turned around and left with Lena.

Staring after her, Shadow didn't know what to think. Letting out a sigh he returned to where Milo was resting. The young tom had evidently been watching him.

"She didn't want to talk, huh?" he observed.

"Nope," Shadow mumbled.

"Well, Dad is making me take your punishment, too. Mom was upset about it, saying it was a bit cruel to go without food, but they both agreed I'm going to sleep outside with you. Dad won on the food issue, too, so I guess we'll have to watch the rest of the clan eat," Milo informed him.

"I'm sorry I got you into this, Milo," Shadow apologized.

"Don't worry about it. I'm the one who suggested it and probably shouldn't have gotten into your fight. I just felt bad when I saw Tonk on top of you, and I reacted without thinking," Milo replied.

"Thanks for backing me, buddy. I think this situation was a learning experience for both of us. Sometimes you have to let comments go because fighting doesn't resolve issues, but only makes things worse. Someone could have gotten badly hurt. Remember, only fight if it is life or death. Don't get your fur ripped out over a girl," Shadow continued smiling.

"Yeah, and don't rub Tonk the wrong way," Milo added, pooting loudly.

Covering his nose with his paw, Shadow held his breath until the smell drifted away. Once he could breathe again, he couldn't help but laugh at Milo.

"Sorry, for some reason I've had gas ever since we ate that trout. I guess it's a good thing I have to sleep outside tonight, though you have to put up with it. Too bad I couldn't have let one rip while I was on top of Tonk. He might have passed out," Milo commented as he and Shadow burst out in laughter.

"Now I know what Tiger was talking about earlier. He asked me if I smelled a dead animal," Shadow revealed.

"Lily and Daisy mentioned something to Momma about it, but I dared not say a word. They would tease me for the rest of my life," Milo giggled.

Still chuckling, the two friends settled down. If nothing else, Shadow was glad to have his friend. At the moment, Milo seemed to be the only one who was on his side. Thinking about the circumstances, he could understand why Angel wasn't talking to him. After all, he had allowed his emotions to get way out of control. Even though Tonk had challenged him and had really started the fight, Shadow felt he still should have handled things differently. In his heart he felt the Creator probably wasn't pleased with his behavior either. There was one thing for certain that came out of this: Tonk liked Angel enough to fight for her. Now he knew Shadow was fighting for her, too.

Chapter Twenty

To Shadow, the last few days had been nerve-racking. So far, the Black Widow Gang hadn't showed up. However, he was pretty sure they were nearby. On top of this, his friends seemed to blame him for the fight. They were nothing like Angel. She refused to talk to him despite his many attempts at conversation. He finally gave up, but he still watched her whenever possible.

Occasionally, she would steal a quick glance in his direction, while covering herself by turning away. Even though Angel was ignoring Shadow, he did have the satisfaction of knowing Tonk was being treated the same way. That alone was worth having Angel avoid him. At least Tonk knew he hadn't won her over and Shadow meant business.

Right now, Shadow was lying on his side giving his black fur coat a good licking. Milo was seated beside him sharpening his claws. Midnight continued to be mad with his son for jumping into the fight, but Cassidy was slowly calming him down.

The rest of the Moonshine Clan was discussing why the gang hadn't attacked them yet. Shadow felt sure they were being watched by Bombay. He dared not say so. Tiger and Midnight had made it clear that Shadow was too hotheaded to make assumptions.

Secretly, Shadow couldn't blame them; he did make a foolish decision. Part of him wished he hadn't fought with Tonk. The other part knew he deserved what he got. He also knew Midnight and Tiger should have known what it was like to have your pride taken away. Shadow hoped the Creator would help him with his crazy thoughts.

As he licked his flank, Shadow noticed Tonk taking a freshly killed trout over to where Angel was seated. Surprisingly, she spoke to the gray tom. Shadow was too far away to hear the words, but whatever was said remained short. After a few moments Tonk left, leaving her to eat the reddish-gray fish. She bent down to take a bite as she glanced over at Shadow.

"I can't believe she's eating the trout! She won't even talk to you, but he seems to get her attention. Somebody needs to poot on him!" exclaimed Milo, rolling his eyes.

Startled by his remark, Shadow only smiled and shook his head. He had almost forgotten Milo was sitting there. Shadow opened his mouth to say something back, but a long yowl made him look up. The yowl had come from Comet, the second in command, while he raced into the center of the clearing. Sandy immediately went to him, knowing it was important.

"The Black Widow Gang is right behind me, Sandy!" Comet announced through gasps of breath.

"Okay, this is it. Mothers and kits are to go to the hiding place. Everyone else needs to prepare for battle. Remember to do the best you can do. I'm proud of all of you. Hopefully the Mighty Creator will help us. Good luck!" Sandy commanded.

Without delay, every member of the Village Cats broke up in small groups. Meanwhile, Shadow went over to where his friends had gathered. Closing their eyes, they asked the Creator for help with the fight and protection for Destiny and the kits.

"Do be careful, Tiger," Destiny begged.

"I will. Now go on with the others," the orange tabby tom replied, gently licking her white forehead.

"Stay out of sight with Destiny, girls. Milo, you are going with your sisters," Cassidy stated firmly.

"But, Momma," Milo started.

Midnight opened his mouth, but Shadow jumped in. He knew Milo wasn't going to listen to his parents without a little persuasion. There had to be a way to talk him into staying with Destiny and his sisters.

"Milo, listen to your mother. This battle is dangerous, and I think you need to stay safe," Shadow declared.

"I can't believe you agree with them. I thought you were on my side," Milo countered, obviously hurt.

"Milo, I am on your side. Think about it. If the gang kills us, at least you can protect your sisters and Destiny. We are counting on you to be brave and to be an example to other young cats who may also need your courage. Whether you realize it or not, we are giving you a dangerous job, and we are confident you will make us proud," Shadow responded.

"Okay, Shadow, I guess you're right," the youngster reluctantly proclaimed.

Turning around, the sand-colored young tom trotted to the designated hiding spot with Daisy, Lily, and Destiny right behind him. Shadow noticed Milo now walked proudly with his head held high and striped tail erect with importance and determination.

"Thanks, Shadow, for convincing Milo to stay with Destiny and the girls. He can be hardheaded sometimes. I'm so glad you thought of a way to make him feel like he's helping out the effort. Also I would like to apologize for giving you a hard time the other day. After thinking it over I realized Tonk probably started the fight. It's not in your character to fight without either being attacked or challenged," Midnight muttered.

"It's okay. I forgive you. Looking back, I know I should have reacted differently," Shadow replied.

The remaining members of the Moonshine Clan gathered together with the Village Cats. Overhead, the half moon had started to shine through a few clouds as the bright stars slowly appeared. Shadow was very mindful of the fact that the growing darkness only meant more danger. The gang could easily sneak up at any time, and it would be harder to spot the enemy.

A twig snapped in the surrounding forest, signaling the arrival of a long-haired silver-gray cat. Shadow instantly recognized the figure as the Black Widow Gang's leader, Bombay.

He wore an evil smirk on his scarred face, as his gaze swept over the group of cats he despised so much. Bombay raised his head up toward the moon and let out a triumphant yowl, acting like he had already won the battle and was the new ruler over the gathered cats.

Out of the darkness came multitudes of cats speeding toward them with equally vicious faces. Shadow had no idea how many cats the Black Widow Gang actually had, and he wondered if they had recruited more members just for this occasion. Now as Shadow looked at the giant mass of enemies coming from all directions, he wasn't so sure they had a chance.

He watched as the gang's leader, Bombay, locked himself into battle with Comet, who had jumped to protect his leader, Sandy. Before Shadow knew it, there were cats fighting everywhere.

From nowhere came a silver-blue tom, which pounced on top of Midnight, knocking the breath out of him. Cassidy ran to his side, sweeping into battle herself. This must have been too much for Tiger, because he found an enemy tomcat and started a fight of his own. Then again, Tiger was almost always looking for a fight, even when there wasn't one.

Shadow didn't have to wait long. He turned around just in time to see Orie, the light brown tom, tackle him from behind. Unfortunately Orie had gained the element of surprise. Although Orie was a rather small-framed cat, Shadow could tell he was very well trained.

The two toms tussled with each other, trying to get a hold on the other one. Shadow finally managed to pin Orie down, only to be flipped onto his back. Orie let out an agitated hiss before snapping his razor-sharp teeth only inches away from Shadow's throat.

A prickle went down Shadow's spine as he realized Orie was fighting until death. Just as the evil brown tom went in for another bite, Angel's friend, Abigail, knocked him off balance. She then locked into battle with Orie, giving Shadow the chance to get up and catch his breath.

Gasping, Shadow stood up and prepared to help Abigail. As he did so, he noticed Angel was fighting with another gang member nearby. The dark tabby tom was approximately twice her size. Shadow remembered him as one of the cats who threatened them and believed his name was Devon. Within minutes, the powerful tom had Angel restrained to the ground and choking for air. Shadow knew he had to do something before it was too late.

Reacting on instinct, he hastily made his way over to the two of them and sunk his jaws into Devon's striped tail. As the giant tom let out an enraged yowl, Shadow backed off, allowing Angel enough room to stand up. Seeing his opponent getting away, Devon lunged on top of her again, nearly knocking her out.

This time he wasn't just attacking her. He was attempting to kill. Before the tom could make contact with Angel's vulnerable neck, Shadow sprung into the air to protect her. Not comprehending what was happening, Shadow had sunk his teeth in Devon's neck. He felt the giant tom's body going limp beneath him, with his blood pouring out onto the ground. Releasing his grip, Shadow started to feel sick on his stomach realizing he had killed Devon. Deep down, he knew he had no other choice, even though he didn't aim to actually kill any cat. For a brief moment, Shadow stood motionless over the dead body, still in shock. Weakly, Angel's voice sounded beside him as she struggled to sit up.

"Thanks, Tonk," she mumbled, still breathing hard.

Shadow couldn't believe his ears. Angel thought Tonk had saved her life instead of him. He was so shocked, he couldn't speak. No matter what he done, Tonk always seemed to get the credit regardless.

After the dust settled around them, Shadow was able to get a closer look at her face in the moonlight. He could tell she was exhausted from the ordeal, but thankful to be alive. Evidently, she was also able to get a better look because her expression changed from gratitude to astonishment and regret.

"Shadow, I—," she began in an apologetic tone.

Angel stopped talking when she was interrupted by a combination of hissing and yowling. Both cats whipped around to see the calico she-cat,

Pixie, dragging Daisy by her front right paw. Screeching in incredible pain, young Daisy was snatched out of the hiding place. Behind her, Milo was trying his best to distract the calico she-cat by puffing up his sand-colored tabby coat in an effort to seem more powerful and scary.

Knowing Milo could only do so much to defend his sister, Shadow rushed over to help him rescue her with Angel behind him. Somehow he managed to detach Pixie's grip from the terrified young she-cat, as Milo pounced on top of his sister's attacker. Between Milo clawing her back and Shadow's swift fighting skills, they were able to corner the calico she-cat. After much fighting, Shadow finally finished her off. Meanwhile, Angel had been trying to comfort poor Daisy the best she could.

"Are you okay, Daisy?" Milo panted when it was all over.

"She'll be fine, but I think her paw might be seriously injured," Angel answered as Daisy cried against her.

"Is everyone else okay?" Shadow implied, looking at Destiny and Lily.

"Yes, I think so," Destiny announced. "That vicious she-cat snuck up on us and attacked me first as we prepared to move to a safer location with the other mothers and kittens. She grabbed Daisy before I could stop her. Milo and Lily jumped in to help me. They are all very brave cats to have stood up to such a brutal she-cat."

Despite Destiny's kind and heartfelt words of praise, Daisy only wailed louder. Shadow feared her paw might be too damaged to save. It obviously was extremely painful, and the horrible experience would take a while to overcome.

All of a sudden, a long yowl came from the clearing, making Shadow jump in fright. Leaving Daisy under Destiny and Lily's care, he walked away from the hiding spot to see what was happening. Angel and Milo went with him in case they were needed.

The scene before them was awful and hard to look at. Shadow wished he had thought to make Milo stay with the she-cats. There were cats lying everywhere, from both the Black Widow Gang and the Village Cats.

Shadow let his gaze sweep over the remaining cats, which were still locked in battle. He desperately hoped Midnight, Cassidy, and Tiger were still alive. So far, he didn't see any sight of them.

"Wow, I'm glad you and Dad made me stay with Destiny. I don't know if I could have handled all this," Milo proclaimed gravely.

Shadow said nothing as he and Angel exchanged a glance. The youngster was right. He couldn't have handled fighting for his life and most certainly could not handle killing another cat. After all, Shadow was barely dealing with the emotional stress of it, although he knew he had no other choice. Angel was probably having some similar feelings of stress since she had almost been killed by Devon.

"Do you think Mom and Dad are okay, Shadow? I can't see them from here. You would think we could at least spot Tiger's orange pelt, but I don't see him either. Maybe we should go find them. They could be really hurt," Milo suggested as he gave Shadow a worried look.

"We need to stay here in case Destiny and your sisters need us, but I'm sure your parents and Tiger are okay. We just have to keep hoping. Try not to worry. The Creator will take care of them," Shadow encouraged him.

Milo slowly nodded, though he wore a concerned expression. Shadow felt bad for him, knowing how hard it must be for such a young cat to deal with the trauma of the battle, the attack on his sister, and his missing parents. He had been through a lot, and Shadow was proud of him for handling it so well. Shadow only hoped Milo's parents were safe. Surprisingly, the youngster pointed his sandy tail up toward the sky.

"Look, the sun is coming up," he softly spoke.

Sure enough, Milo was right. The morning sun was slowly rising above the mountains in the distance. Morning was on its way, no matter what any cat thought. Shadow was glad to see it, knowing they could at least see their enemies in the sunlight. He was amazed at how fast time had passed overnight. Now as it was steadily getting lighter, more and more cats were stopping to look up at the sunrise.

Shadow noticed that some cats looked at the sun in horror. They were slowly gathering together. Among them were Orie, Scarlet, and Bengal, the second in command. That's when Shadow comprehended that the cluster of cats were in fact the remaining members of the Black Widow Gang. The arrival of the sun had evidently made them realize how outnumbered they were.

Before Shadow knew what had happened, Bengal led the rest of his leader's gang out of the clearing and headed for the surrounding mountains. Seeing their evil opponents getting away, some of the Village Cats chased them to the bend of the river eager to finish them once and for all.

"Let them go!" exclaimed Sandy from her perch on a rock. Then she added, "Their leader, Bombay, is dead. It will take Bengal awhile to get his new gang together, but with their leader gone I don't think we will hear from them again."

Relief flooded over Shadow as he heard Sandy's words. More than anything he hoped she was right. Now that Bombay was dead, things would hopefully get better.

"Milo, go tell Destiny the battle is over. Then I want you to help Lily get Daisy and Destiny down to the reeds so they can rest and we can check her injury. Meanwhile I'm going to go look for your parents and Tiger," Shadow instructed.

"Come on, Milo, I'll help you," Angel offered as the two of them headed for the bushes where the she-cats were hiding.

Watching them go, Shadow wondered if Angel was still mad at him. Sighing, he made his way down the small hill and into the clearing. Being careful not to fall over the dead cats, he searched the faces of the survivors. From a distance he could barely make out a sand-colored tabby and a solid black tom as they embraced on the opposite side of the clearing. At the same moment an orange-striped cat approached them. Shadow's heart surged with happiness as he recognized the cats. Carefully picking up his pace, he trotted toward his friends, knowing they were no doubt exhausted and possibly even injured. But thanks to the Creator, they were alive!

Chapter Twenty-One

Ever since the violent battle with the Black Widow Gang, the Moonshine Clan and the Village Cats had been hard at work cleaning up the clearing. Almost every cat had suffered some kind of injury. Some had barely escaped with their lives. In fact, the clearing beside the river had been covered with bodies, from both the Black Widow Gang and the Village Cats. Luckily, most of the Moonshine Clan only had cuts and bruises, but Daisy's paw was indeed unfixable.

Angel's friend Lena looked at Daisy's paw, but sadly there wasn't anything she could do except wrap it in spiderwebs and give her poppy seeds for pain. Lena had been working with her to slowly relearn how to walk again. Although every step she took was painful, she was making some progress. At first, Daisy refused to do anything until she realized how lucky she really was. So many cats weren't half as lucky.

It took several days to bury the ones who didn't make it. Shadow had helped dig so many holes he couldn't count them all. To him it was depressing to bury the cats he had grown used to seeing.

The worst one was Angel's friend, Abigail. Evidently, the silver-blue she-cat had lost her courageous battle with Orie. Deep down, Shadow felt it should have been him being buried. After all, Abigail had jumped in to help when the tom was trying to kill him. If he hadn't been trying to protect Angel, he could have helped her and she wouldn't have been killed.

He tried to keep telling himself it just wasn't his fault, but it still hurt to see the tears in Angel's and Lena's eyes.

Unfortunately the situation with Angel still hadn't been resolved. Angel had thanked Shadow for saving her life from Devon and apologized for automatically thinking he was Tonk. Shadow had, of course, forgiven her while offering his heartfelt sorrow for the loss of her friend Abigail. However, when Shadow began to bring up the fight with Tonk, Angel said she didn't want to talk about it until she had more time to mourn. Without thinking, Shadow had insisted they discuss the fight because he was afraid Tonk would convince her to stay in the village. This point did not go over well with Angel, who accused him of being uncaring and insensitive. Since then she hadn't spoken to him, leaving Shadow feeling frustrated with himself for pushing her away.

Once the clearing by the river had been cleaned up, the two clans moved back to the Village Cats' base near the human shelters. Right now, everyone was waiting for Sandy to call a meeting. She was going to discuss potential rules and regulations for the future. Surprisingly, she decided to allow the Moonshine Clan the opportunity to voice their opinion on what the new rules should be.

Shadow licked his black fur as he waited for Sandy's meeting. From where he sat, he watched Sandy and Comet leave the tall grass and approach the Moonshine Clan. He stood up to greet them, signaling with his long black tail for the rest of the clan to do the same. Comet let out a yowl to call the Village Cats together. Once he had their attention, Sandy cleared her throat.

"As you know, it has been several days since the gang attacked us. It is time to make some rules for each of our clans to live by. First, I think we must lay down territory rights. How about the bend of the river being the boundary? Since you helped us fight off the gang there I feel like it would be honorable for us to mark the area in remembrance of those who were injured and who lost their lives fighting for our freedom," Sandy proclaimed.

"Okay, sounds fair," Midnight replied, while the rest of the Moonshine Clan nodded in agreement.

"Very well. That part of the river is yours and the village is ours. I feel like we can trust you, but if for any reason members of your clan threaten us or attack us, you will no longer be welcome. This goes for our clan as well. I would hope no cat belonging to my clan would threaten you," Sandy declared.

The sand-colored tabby leader paused to gaze sharply at the cats who had gathered around her to listen to the rules. This silent warning seemed to penetrate through the Village Cats as if each fully understood what punishment they would receive if they disobeyed. Interestingly enough, her eyes lingered in Tonk's direction for a longer amount of time, clearly singling him out.

"If you need us for anything just come to me and ask, just as I will do for you. Comet is the second in command, which means if something were to happen to me, he is the new leader. He has witnessed what you have done for us and will always treat you with respect," Sandy continued.

"I promise I won't forget the kindness you have shown. If for any reason I would have to take Sandy's place, which I don't plan on doing, you would be treated fairly," Comet added.

At this point Shadow heard Tonk snort in disapproval. Looking at him, he wondered if he would say anything knowing he wasn't pleased with the new arrangements. Strangely the tom seemed to keep his mouth shut as Comet sent him a nasty look.

"When winter comes and there isn't much food, each clan can ask the other for fresh meat. If they don't ask, the other clan has the right to do what they please with the intruder. Do you agree with the rules I have suggested?" Sandy questioned.

"They sound pretty good to me," Tiger declared.

"Yes, I think these rules will do everyone justice," Midnight agreed.

"Good! Now with the rules in place, I would like to thank you on behalf of the Village Cats. If there is anything we can do for you before you leave tomorrow, let me know," Sandy announced, smiling broadly.

Afterward, the tabby leader made her way back to the pile of fresh meat in the center of the base. Comet followed her immediately, stopping long enough to speak to one of his fellow clan mates. Watching them go, Shadow noticed Angel and her friend Lena talking quietly together at the edge of the tall green grass where the cats slept. They were, no doubt, reminiscing about the times they spent with their beloved best friend, Abigail.

Shadow wanted to go over and talk to Angel, but he knew she still did not wish to speak to him. More than anything else, he wanted her to know how much he cared about her and how sorry he was for being pushy. He knew the Moonshine Clan would soon be leaving for the farm. Sadly he had doubts as to whether she would be coming with them.

Ever since they had returned from the mountain, Angel had been eating and sleeping with her friends. Shadow wasn't so sure she still wanted to be a member of the Moonshine Clan. Deep down in his soul, he didn't think he could walk away from her again. The last time he said good-bye, it nearly killed him. He had repeatedly asked the Creator what he needed to do but hadn't received a clear answer. Watching her, Shadow's heart suddenly indicated that he should do something.

Before Shadow could follow through with his plan, Milo came up to him and sat down. At first Shadow said nothing as he debated whether he should discuss his thoughts with his friend. Not wanting any regrets, he decided to ask Milo's opinion before jumping to do something that would ultimately affect their friendship.

"Milo, I need to ask you an important question. Considering the events of the last few days, do you suppose Angel will choose to stay here with her friends or go home with us?" Shadow inquired.

For a few moments, Milo wore a surprised look as if he wasn't sure what Shadow meant. However, after some thought the young tom seemed to understand what Shadow was trying to say.

"Well, now that you mention it, Angel does seem to be having second thoughts," Milo answered. After a brief silence, he added, "You have to do what you think is best, Shadow. I'll support you no matter which decision you select."

"Thanks, Milo," Shadow muttered.

Leaving his young friend, Shadow made his way over to where Sandy and Comet were eating their fresh kill. As he walked, he overheard Midnight asking Milo where he was going. Shockingly, Milo gave his dad a generic answer without saying anything about their discussion. Once Shadow got to where Sandy was sitting, he patiently waited for her to notice him. He knew there was only one thing he could do to live a happy life.

"Yes, Shadow, is there something on your mind?" the tabby leader questioned once she spotted him waiting to speak with her.

Shadow took a deep breath, knowing the question he was preparing to ask would change not only his life but also those he cared about the most. Standing tall and proud, Shadow told her his request.

"Well, you said if there was anything you could do for us, all we had to do was ask," he began. "I would like to have your approval to join your clan."

Sandy was silent as she glanced at Comet, who was seated beside her. She appeared to be carefully thinking over his unexpected decision. As Shadow waited patiently, he noticed that several cats had stopped to see what they were doing. Before long, every cat in the base was listening to the conversation, including the Moonshine Clan.

Cautiously Sandy spoke. "I see. Are you sure this is your wish? I thought your clan was close to each other."

"We are close friends, but after thinking it over I have decided I would rather stay here and join the Village Cats," Shadow explained.

"What about your obligations for the Moonshine Clan?" Sandy implied curiously.

"Lily, Daisy, and Milo are almost grown cats now, and they are able to help out. Plus, we are expecting a new set of kittens soon," he indicated.

"Well, if this is your desire—," Sandy began, but she was rudely interrupted by a furious yowl.

Looking to see who spoke up, Shadow realized the yowl came from Angel. She was trotting determinedly over to them from the edge of the clearing. Obviously she didn't like what she had overheard.

"Shadow, what do you think you're doing? Have you lost your mind? Why in the world are you leaving your clan?" Angel demanded in disbelief.

"Angel, I have already made my decision. There isn't anything you can do to change my mind. I don't have a choice," he replied calmly.

"You don't have a choice? Yeah, right! All I know is, you are only thinking of yourself!" she stated firmly.

Angel whipped around and headed back to where Lena was seated. Watching her go, Shadow decided to tell her the things she needed to hear. After all, this could be his last opportunity to let her know how he truly felt. If nothing else, he could at least get things off his chest.

"I do care about somebody besides myself, Angel. I care about my friends and I care about you," he countered.

Angel froze when she heard his words. She turned back to face him with a hurt look in her eyes.

"No, Shadow, if you care about me at all, you wouldn't have fought with Tonk. I don't know why you did it or why you are leaving your clan. They aren't just your friends, they are your family. You said Milo was like your little brother, but I'm not so sure. I just don't understand why!" she expressed.

"Because I love you!" he blurted out.

Before realizing it, Shadow had accidentally revealed his personal and heartfelt feelings in front of her clan and his. As the words left his mouth he felt an overwhelming sense of embarrassment and was awkwardly aware of the blown-away looks on the faces of those around him.

"Whoa, unbelievable," mumbled Tiger in a hushed voice.

Angel was now staring at him wide-eyed with shock. Shadow was so humiliated he hung his head. He never liked being in the spotlight or the center of attention. This time Tonk shouldered his way through the crowd wearing a look of disgust on his face.

"You have got to be kidding me! I can't believe my ears! He's only saying these mushy, lovey-dovey things so you'll go with him. Truthfully, he probably doesn't even care that you want to stay here with your friends," Tonk declared hotly.

"Stay out of this, Tonk. This has nothing to do with you. It is strictly between Shadow and me," Angel muttered.

"But—," Tonk began as she cut him off again.

"Stop it, Tonk!" Angel insisted, giving him a stern look.

Turning her attention back to Shadow, Angel gave him a look of regret. She clearly felt bad about unloading on him in front of everyone.

"I had no idea you felt this way, Shadow. You were actually going to give up the life you've worked hard to have just to be with me?" she questioned him.

Shadow opened his mouth to reply, but Sandy jumped in.

"Look, I don't mean to be rude; however, I think this is a private conversation. Therefore, everyone must go back to their duties, and yes, Tonk, that means you, too. Comet, if anyone disobeys you, please bring them to me," she announced, walking through the gathered cats toward her sleeping quarters.

With a lot of groans, the crowd slowly retreated, though some took their precious time. Tonk was the last one to go, leaving Comet with no choice but to supervise his departure. Unfortunately this had to be done by force, since Tonk was keen on staying. Once he had been restrained, he was hauled away.

"Let go of me! I have as much a right to stay as that worthless, pathetic pipsqueak!" Tonk shouted angrily as four cats struggled with him. "You're going to regret crossing me, Shadow. You don't know what the consequences of this will be!"

After the four cats and Comet had managed to somewhat control Tonk, Shadow approached Angel so that they could talk more privately. He overheard Comet ordering for Tonk to be guarded until he cooled off. Trying to ignore Tonk's continuous yelling and threats, he again attempted to speak.

"Yes, I am willing to change clans in order to stay here with you. I'm sorry I fought with Tonk and for never telling you how much you mean to me, but I wasn't sure how to go about it. I just know I can't bear to lose you again," he proclaimed.

"Shadow, I should be the one saying sorry. I shouldn't have blamed you for fighting with Tonk. Hopefully you can find it in your heart to forgive me," she pleaded, hanging her head.

"Of course I forgive you, Angel. You have no idea how relieved I am to know you aren't mad with me," he insisted, smiling.

"Well, as grateful as I am to know you are willing to change clans to make me happy, I still want to stay with your clan. There is something special about the Moonshine Clan, and I feel like I belong in it," Angel continued.

Shadow smiled as his heart pounded against his chest in happiness. Things couldn't be better; Angel had decided to be with him. Stepping forward, he gently gave her forehead a lick of affection.

"Welcome back, Angel," he muttered tenderly.

Walking side by side, Shadow and Angel went over to the edge of the tall green grass where the Moonshine Clan was resting. As they approached the clan, young Milo cleared his throat.

"So, did you two work things out?" he questioned.

"You don't have to worry. I talked Shadow into remaining a mountain cat," Angel responded with a smile.

"Does that mean you're going to stay with us, too?" Daisy wanted to know.

"Yeah, I think I am," Angel replied.

At this point Angel's friends, Lena and Marcus, came over to them. Both of them had evidently overheard Angel because they wore sad looks on their faces.

"Sounds like you're planning to leave, huh?" Lena implied dejectedly.

"Oh, Lena, I know you want me to stay, but I just can't. My life is with the Moonshine Clan and Shadow. I wish you would come with me, though," Angel responded.

"I understand you have to follow your heart, but I don't think I can leave right now. I'm just going to miss you," the light gray she-cat declared.

Angel went over to her best friend and rubbed against her lovingly. Feeling bad for the three friends, Shadow had an idea. Knowing his own friends wouldn't mind, he decided to be generous to Lena and Marcus by asking them to join their group.

"Why don't the two of you eat with us tonight? We would be honored to have you," Shadow kindly suggested.

Lena and Marcus exchanged a look of surprise while staring at him in total bewilderment. Obviously, they were caught off guard by the offer. Finally Lena spoke up as she gave him a shy smile.

"We don't want to intrude, but it would be nice to spend time with Angel—especially since you are going to leave out tomorrow," she agreed.

"Yeah, thanks for inviting us. It really means a lot. Sorry for the way Tonk acted. I still can't believe he disobeyed Sandy and totally freaked out," Marcus added softly.

Shadow only nodded, not wanting to cause trouble by commenting on Tonk's insane behavior. While the cats settled down, Tiger and Midnight brought over enough fresh meat for everyone to eat. Then they thanked the Creator for the food. When they were finished with their tasty meal of mice and squirrels, they told stories of past adventures until the stars appeared. Since it was so late, Lena and Marcus asked to sleep with them to be with Angel. They slept among the tall grass lining the edge of the base.

Midnight and Cassidy slept side by side, as their two daughters cuddled close to them. Destiny stretched out on the opposite side of Cassidy, with Tiger on her right side. Usually Milo stretched out beside Shadow, but this time he left enough room for Angel, Lena, and Marcus.

It surprised Shadow at how thoughtful Milo was becoming. Instead of taking up a lot of room like he normally did, he was considerate of others. Whether the youngster realized it or not, he was acting more and more like a grown tomcat and less like a mere kit.

Situating himself, Shadow allowed Angel to get comfortable while Lena and Marcus positioned themselves on her opposite side. Having Angel so close to him felt wonderful, particularly since she had ignored him for almost a half a moon. Pondering over the trials he had been through, Shadow was thankful the Creator was there to make everything work out. He felt proud he hadn't allowed Tonk to cause him to lose his temper and fight like he had done before. Shadow was also glad Angel had chosen to stay with him so he wouldn't have to leave his own family. It felt good to have finally forgiven each other and to renew their relationship. Exhausted, Shadow slowly drifted off into a deep sleep with Angel's black and white fur intermixed with his.

Chapter Twenty-Two

Breathing heavily Shadow made his way up the slippery slope. The mixture of rain and wind was pounding him the whole time he tried to climb up the side of the mountain. Midnight and Tiger were in the lead, making sure the path was stable enough to hold the rest of the clan. Behind them, Cassidy and Angel walked on each side of Destiny. She was having a hard time, being so close to kittening her first litter. Lily followed the older she-cats, walking close to her sister Daisy, who was having trouble climbing. Trailing the group was Shadow and Milo.

It had been decided that they would go last to stop Destiny and Daisy from falling down off of the mountain. Shadow knew if either of them lost control of their grip, they wouldn't survive the fall, especially considering that all of the rocks down below looked very sharp.

By now, his paw pads were sore and bloody from the long haul over what seemed to be hundreds of massive boulders. Shadow figured everyone had the same issues, but so far no one complained. He had no idea how far he and his friends had actually gone, but he figured they had to be getting close to the top.

Several days had passed since the Moonshine Clan said their good-byes to their Village Cat friends. The departure was a sad one, particularly for Angel and Lena. Shadow knew Angel was having trouble dealing with her mixed emotions. She clearly missed Lena and Marcus already, although she tried to hide her feelings. He only hoped the trip back home somewhat got her mind off of the heartache.

Of course Tonk had showed himself when they were preparing to leave. He had begged and pleaded with Angel to stay and didn't take it well when she refused. In fact he again started to threaten Shadow, and Sandy was forced to have him restrained. Shadow had no idea how long Sandy would keep him under security, but he knew there was a possibility Tonk would follow them since he knew the way to their home on the mountain.

As Shadow trailed behind the rest of the clan, he noticed Daisy kept stumbling on the loose dirt and small rocks. Just then, the young she-cat slipped, shrieking in terror as she tried to claw the rocks.

"Help! Help! Shadow, catch me!" Daisy screamed.

Reacting quickly, Shadow grabbed her by the scruff of her neck and helped her back onto the rocky boulder.

Once she was safe she panted, "Thanks, I didn't think I was going to make it."

Hearing the screaming, Cassidy turned to see Shadow catching her daughter. Concerned, she and Midnight came over to see if Daisy was alright. Noticing she was breathing hard and wincing in pain from her injured leg, Cassidy turned to Midnight.

"We need to stop and find some shelter. Daisy is having a hard time keeping up, and her paw is giving her quite a bit of pain. We should probably rewrap it in spiderwebs. In fact we all should wrap our bloody paw pads," she advised in a worried tone.

"I agree. How about the birch tree over there?" Midnight suggested.

Nodding her approval, Cassidy helped Daisy over to the tree while Angel and Lily assisted Destiny. The massive birch luckily had been hollowed out either naturally or by some other animal. Once the Moonshine Clan made their way over to the tree, they filed inside. While Angel helped Destiny get situated, Cassidy found some spiderwebs. Very carefully, she rewrapped Daisy's paw, then she took the remainder and applied them to her other bloody paws and to Destiny's.

"I'm sure you guys are hungry. Why don't we go catch everyone something to eat, Midnight?" Tiger questioned.

"That's a good idea. I'll look for some of those poppy seeds, too. Daisy might need them for pain," Midnight replied, following Tiger back out into the downpour.

"Come on, Milo. Let's go hunting with them," Shadow suggested.

With a quick nod of agreement, Milo started back out behind Tiger and his father. To Shadow's complete surprise, Angel followed them. Tilting his head, he gave her a questioning look.

"I'm going, too," she announced with a determined look on her face.

Shadow could tell she was going regardless of what he thought or said, so he just motioned for her to go next. After the group was out into the vast forest, the five of them split up. When Shadow trotted off toward some blackberry bushes, he heard a rustling of leaves behind him. Turning around he allowed his dark green eyes to scan the forest for the animal making the noise. Shockingly, the sweet scent he picked up was Angel's.

"Come on out, Angel. Why are you following me? We were supposed to be hunting alone, remember?" Shadow related.

Very reluctantly, Angel emerged from the bushes with an embarrassed look on her face. She glanced around nervously as if she were expecting to see someone else appear. Her behavior was rather unusual, and Shadow wondered what was causing it.

"Shadow, I didn't mean to sneak around like this, but I really need to talk to you," Angel urged as she absentmindedly flexed her claws into the wet ground.

"As much as I want to stay here and chat, I can't. The clan is hungry, and we have to go back with some fresh kill," he declared.

"There is something you need to know, Shadow. It has been bothering me, but I don't want to discuss it with the others. Please listen. I promise it won't take long," she pleaded desperately.

For a few moments, Shadow just stared at her. He knew he should be hunting, but she obviously had something important to say. Knowing Angel was evidently distressed, Shadow dipped his head signaling for her to continue. Whatever she had on her mind was obviously difficult to say, because she was constantly kneading the ground in front of her with extended claws.

"Shadow, I wanted to clear something up," she stammered uneasily.

"Like what?" Shadow prompted, a bit confused.

"It is custom at home, I mean at the base, for a tom to claim a she-cat. This way, there are less fights. If the she-cat accepts the offer, the two are considered off limits," she explained.

"So what does all this have to do with our relationship? The Moonshine Clan doesn't have those rules," Shadow wanted to know.

"I feel like I should have told you before now. Tonk has claimed me in the past. Over time I lost count, but I never said yes," Angel revealed.

"Okay, I'm glad you told me; however, I'm still confused. Tonk isn't here so there is no reason for you to feel uncomfortable," Shadow pointed out.

"That's true, but I still think it would be wise to follow my clan's rule because Tonk won't honor our relationship if we don't. For example, if we ever went back to visit my old clan I would be considered available," she hinted.

"Well, if it makes you feel better I'm willing to do this claim thing. What do we have to do?" Shadow inquired.

"Nothing really, I mean, you've kind of done it already. When you said you loved me in front of everyone, it was considered a claim. Now all I have to do to make the claim official is accept. So as of today I accept your claim. I love you, Shadow," Angel announced quietly.

Shadow smiled at her. "I love you, too, Angel. I'm glad you explained this to me, though I must say, here my only competition is Milo. I don't think we have to worry," he replied laughing.

Angel also laughed at the silly suggestion. Then she gave him a serious look.

"Shadow, I really do care about you. I know I can trust you completely. You have done so much for me over these past few moons," she muttered.

"I feel the same way about you. Come on, let's go back to the birch tree before it rains again," he declared.

Leading the way through the downpour, Shadow trotted back to the birch tree with Angel by his side. When the two of them got there, Midnight, Tiger, and Milo had returned with a generous amount of fresh meat. Suddenly Shadow realized with a sickening feeling he and Angel hadn't even attempted to hunt for the clan. The humiliating sensation in the pit of his stomach only got worse as Midnight and Tiger came to the same conclusion.

"Where is your kill?" Midnight questioned suspiciously.

"I, well, we sort of—," Shadow started with Tiger cutting him off.

"Don't give us excuses. Those mice almost hunted themselves today. Any cat even thinking about food could have taken down several mice in a matter of a few seconds. You didn't even try to hunt, did you?" Tiger confronted him.

"No, but—," Shadow began; however, he was again interrupted.

"Shadow, you and Angel were supposed to be helping us kill enough fresh mice for everyone to eat. What is this behavior teaching Milo?" Midnight countered.

This time Angel spoke up. "It was totally my fault, guys. Shadow was trying hard to hunt, but I needed to talk to him. The situation was rather urgent."

"Talking was so important you forgot your duty to the clan?" Tiger insisted.

"Yes, when it's our relationship! You two should know how important a relationship is," Angel answered sharply.

Milo watched with wide, yellow eyes at the bickering adults. He wore an expression of both confusion and understanding, as if the youngster was trying to figure out which party was right.

"You know, this is completely outrageous," Shadow stated angrily. "We have plenty of fresh kill for everybody, so who's complaining? And don't go blaming Angel; I'm glad we had a chance to talk privately."

"Why couldn't you talk some other time? Was it necessary to chitchat while we were trying to hunt?" Tiger demanded.

"I admit the timing was off, but the conversation was definitely necessary. Me and Angel are a couple, no thanks to you," Shadow responded bitterly.

Before Tiger or anyone else could say a word, Lily's black pelt came running out of the hollowed-out tree. Her sandy-white sister, Daisy, hobbled close behind, wincing as she walked on her injured leg.

"Destiny is having her kittens!" Lily shouted gleefully.

"Momma sent us to get you, Tiger, and you, too, Angel," Daisy added.

Angel immediately jumped up but stopped to wait for Tiger to go in first. Tiger just stood where he was, completely stunned by the news. Very slowly, the orange tabby tom moved forward, appearing to shake like a newborn kit learning to walk. Shadow sympathized with him, realizing Tiger was about to become a father. Even though they were disagreeing just a few moments ago, he needed to forgive him for his previous words and actions.

Once Tiger and Angel had entered the hollowed-out tree, Shadow settled down. Surprisingly, Midnight said nothing more about Shadow's confession. The solid black tom was busy getting Daisy to eat the poppy seeds for her pain. Afterward, he sat and listened to his daughters discuss the new names of the kittens.

Self-consciously, Shadow noticed Milo staring at him. As the two friends made eye contact, the young tom got up and trotted over. Unnoticed by the others, Milo gave him a serious look.

"Shadow, you are my best friend, but I know I have to share you with Angel. I just don't want to lose our relationship," he muttered.

"Oh, Milo, you don't have to worry about our friendship. We will always be buddies, no matter where life takes us. One day you will find a she-cat who loves you just as much as Angel loves me," Shadow replied smiling.

"Yeah, right. She-cats are way too complicated to figure out," Milo declared with a chuckle.

Shadow smiled at the youngster. As if their conversation had summoned her, Angel came from within the tree trunk.

"You can come see the kittens now," she told them.

One by one, the five cats filed in behind Angel. Shadow was eager to meet the new members of the Moonshine Clan. He had of course been looking forward to seeing them, especially knowing how much he cared about Lily, Daisy, and Milo. It had occurred to him he would never be as close to them as he was with Milo. They had something special.

As the clan entered the hollowed-out birch tree, Shadow saw Destiny's white-furred body lying on some moss. Tiger was seated beside her with Cassidy on her opposite side. While everyone was settling around Destiny, Shadow was able to see four tiny kittens as they blindly nuzzled against their mother. Shadow exchanged a smile with her, recalling the talks they had back in the forest and of Destiny's desire for a family like Cassidy's one day. Her dream came true, and Shadow felt happy to share in his dear friend's excitement.

"Hey, guys, the Creator blessed us with four kittens," Tiger proclaimed happily.

"Yeah, let me introduce you to them," Destiny suggested proudly.

She gently touched the first two kittens with her muzzle. They were both exact images of their father, Tiger, wearing the same orange tabby coat.

"Tiger and I have already given them names. There are three boys and a little girl. These two are Chase and Hunter. Although they look like twins this one has a white spot between his toes on the right paw. We decided to name him Hunter since we had to hunt for it. I don't know how we're going to be able to keep them apart without always looking for the spot," Destiny announced enthusiastically.

The next kit she touched was white with orange splotches along his back.

"We named this one Bo," she added.

"And this little sweetheart is Poppy," continued Tiger, nodding toward the tiny kit on the end of the row.

The teeny-tiny she-cat had light orange fur with no stripes. Shadow could tell Tiger was almost beside himself with pride, and this was quite understandable. He wondered if these four kittens would be mischievous like Midnight's were. If they were anything like Milo, Tiger was going to have his paws full.

"They are so cute!" Angel exclaimed.

"I agree, and we are so blessed that they are healthy considering all you've been through. The Creator was definitely with you. I can't believe you are a new mother. Speaking of Poppy, did you find any poppy seeds, Midnight?" Cassidy mentioned.

"Yep, and Daisy already took it while you helped Destiny. She can have what's left if she needs it. I don't mean to change the subject, but I'm curious. Did I hear you say we have a new couple?" Midnight questioned as he looked at Shadow expectantly.

Strangely enough, Shadow at first had no idea what he was talking about, but it soon dawned on him. A little embarrassed, he realized Midnight was smiling at him in amusement while Milo, Daisy, and Lily giggled.

"Oh, yeah, we're a couple now," Shadow responded awkwardly.

"Okay, is there something we missed?" Cassidy implied.

"Shadow and Angel have finally admitted they are either going together or are a couple. At this point what does it matter? After what happened in the village I thought it was pretty obvious, but apparently I'm the only one who saw it coming. I guess they still needed time to realize they were in love. I personally figured out they were lovebirds moons ago," Milo answered with a snicker.

"Congratulations!" exclaimed Destiny.

"Thanks," Angel replied shyly.

"Enough lovey-dovey stuff. I'm hungry. When are we going to eat?" Lily burst out, bouncing in excitement.

Everyone laughed at this question. So much was going on they had forgotten to eat. Somehow this didn't matter much. The events of the day were too chaotic to remember the simple things in life.

"Leave it to Lily to remember food! I'll go get the fresh kill," Shadow offered, making his way outside.

"Let me help you," Milo volunteered, following him.

Heading back out, Shadow and Milo exited the hollowed tree. Meanwhile, Cassidy and Angel worked on wrapping everyone's bloody paw pads with spiderwebs, leaving enough for Milo and Shadow to wrap theirs. Outside the rainy weather had pretty much stopped and the wind wasn't nearly as bad. Walking over to the pile of fresh kill, Milo bent down and picked up several mice by their tails. Then the young tom carried his load back to the others. Just as Shadow was about to do the same he noticed they were close to a cliff. With all of the hard rain, the clan had overlooked this dangerous hazard.

Knowing he and his friends needed to stay here until Destiny and the kits could travel, he decided to have a look. Going over to the massive boulders, Shadow peered down over the edge. The view was gorgeous, much like the view from the farmhouse. From here, Shadow could see the village and the forest down below. A beautiful, multicolored rainbow stood high above the valley, arching beyond the mountains in the distance. Shadow recalled seeing a rainbow the day they were forced to leave their beloved forest.

Looking at it, Shadow felt the Creator was giving him this sign of hope as a reminder of the many blessings He had given them throughout their amazing journey. Beginning from their forest home in the spring to their newfound home in the mountains they had been challenged to trust the Creator in so many different ways.

After every bad rainstorm there always seems to be a rainbow, Shadow thought. *We lost our home and everything we had, but we stuck together and look at us today. If the humans hadn't taken our home away, I would have never met Angel.*

Shadow was beginning to understand you could find something good out of bad situations. Between the humans taking over their forest home and the horrific battle with the Black Widow Gang they had been through a lot. The adventure had caused them to travel for over five moons while caring for Milo, Daisy, and Lily, including trying to find a safe place to live. In addition the clan had grown again by adding four new kittens—a dream his dear friend Destiny had shared with him so many moons ago.

Thinking back, Shadow reflected on all the numerous adversities they had faced and the lessons learned. It felt good to finally have peace.

Most importantly he now had a close relationship with Angel, though he doubted Tonk was going to give up trying to change Angel's mind.

That's when it struck him that the clan needed to discuss the remaining members of the Black Widow Gang. What if they decided to seek revenge? Sandy seemed to think there was no need to worry; however, it wouldn't hurt to consider the possibility of another attack.

Oh, well, he pondered, *we'll tackle this storm if it comes. For right now, we are safe and there is no reason to concern everyone until we are home. Getting the newborn kits to the farm will be a complicated task in itself.*

Smiling broadly, Shadow turned around and picked up the remaining mouthful of mouse tails. With overwhelming hope surging in his heart, he made his way back to the hollowed-out tree where his dearly loved family waited.

Character Values

Shadow and his friends learn many lessons through their adventures. Look at the list and see if you can remember when and how these characteristics came into play. Which ones have you learned?

<table>
<tr><td>✓ Hope</td><td>✓ Love</td></tr>
<tr><td>✓ Faith</td><td>✓ Trust</td></tr>
<tr><td>✓ Friendship</td><td>✓ Respect</td></tr>
<tr><td>✓ Obeying parents</td><td>✓ Wisdom and knowledge</td></tr>
<tr><td>✓ Survival skills</td><td>✓ Sacrifice and protection</td></tr>
<tr><td>✓ Truthfulness and honesty</td><td>✓ Grief and loss</td></tr>
<tr><td>✓ Families working together</td><td>✓ Suffering and illness</td></tr>
<tr><td>✓ Counting blessings</td><td>✓ Don't lie</td></tr>
<tr><td>✓ Don't have fear</td><td>✓ Don't argue</td></tr>
<tr><td>✓ Don't be jealous</td><td>✓ Don't get angry and fight</td></tr>
<tr><td>✓ Don't eavesdrop</td><td>✓ Don't be prideful or arrogant</td></tr>
</table>

"But the fruit of the Spirit is love, joy, peace, longsuffering, kindness, goodness, faithfulness, gentleness, self-control."

GALATIANS 5:22–23

Get the Scoop

Cool Facts for Your Adventure

- Shadow, Midnight, Cassidy, Tiger, and Destiny are real wild cats I encountered in the mountains. Sandy and Comet are pets my family has had over the years. Angel is our current pet. Like her character, she is spunky and loves having fun.
- Girl cats are called she-cats, and boys are toms. Kittens are also called kits.
- Cats, like dogs, come in all kinds of breeds. Some characters were given names of different breeds. Tonk (Tonkinese), Bombay (Bombay), Bengal (Bengal), Devon (Devon Rex), Orie (Oriental Shorthair).
- Mom cats (also called queens) usually raise their kittens alone. Toms leave their families and never see them again. In this book the cats remain a family.
- A litter is a family of baby kittens born at the same time, such as Milo, Daisy, and Lily. The average number of kittens in a litter is four, but survival depends on the health of the kits and the living conditions of the mother. It usually takes nine weeks for a she-cat to have kittens.
- Cats living in the wild usually have a new litter once a year, while domestic cats can have up to three litters a year. Wild cats don't always have the same two parents because the dad leaves. In this book the parents stay together to care for their kits.
- Kittens are born blind, deaf, and helpless. After birth, their mother licks them to clean their tiny bodies and get their blood flowing through them. Kittens begin to see and hear in about ten days. (Blue-eyed white cats usually remain deaf. Although Destiny is white, she has yellow eyes, so she can hear.)

- Kittens nurse, or drink their mother's milk, until they are weaned (about five weeks from birth). They can leave their mom at around six weeks old. When they are between six and twelve months old, they can have kittens of their own.

- It's nearly impossible to prove that cats or dogs have identical twins. Most identical twins have some kind of marking somewhere on their bodies telling them apart (even a speck between their toes or in their ears)!

- Mother cats carry their kittens by the scruff of their neck. The scruff is the loose skin at the back of their necks. It enables them to be carried until they learn to walk, which takes about three weeks. Being carried by the scruff of their neck doesn't hurt them.

- Cats are digitigrade, which means they walk on their toes. They also walk or run by moving their front and back legs on the right side, then moving the front and back legs on the left side. Only two other animals do this: the camel and the giraffe.

- Cats' bodies are like elastic; they are powerful and amazing creatures. God made them in a special way so that their spines allow them to bend and flex. If they fall, they almost always land on their paws. They have tiny muscles attached to their hair, enabling them to bristle all over.

- Unlike our fingernails and toenails, a cat's claw is connected to the last bone on the toes. A muscle makes the claw unsheathe (or come out). All cats except cheetahs have this weapon. To "sheathe" means to cover a sword or knife with a protective case. "Sheathe" can also describe the way cat claws retract or are covered by skin.

- Most people think black cats are unlucky. Actually they don't get as many diseases and therefore typically live longer. That's pretty lucky!

- God made cats' eyes to see extremely well in the darkness. The pupil (the black part of the eye) enlarges to allow in more light. Cats' pupils do this at night and when hunting. The pupil becomes a small slit when cats are more relaxed or during the daylight hours. Typically, cats can't see colors well, but in this book they do have the ability.

- A cat's sense of smell and touch is sharp. Their eyebrows, whiskers, cheek fur, and ear hair are sensitive to vibrations. Even their nose tip, toes, and paws are sensitive. Their ears have about thirty muscles (humans have six). This gives them the ability to turn their ears in different directions and makes them skilled hunters.

- Cats use their tail and body to express emotions and personality. Cats rub against objects and other cats to mark them with their scent to claim ownership. (That's why they rub against you—to tell other cats, "Hey, this kid is mine!") Tomcats also spray their urine on things so other toms know whose territory it is.

- The tongue of a cat has sharp, backward pointing spines near the tip. To us the tongue feels rough, but to cats it's a big help. The sharpness enables them to groom their fur easier and helps lap up water quicker. Cats love to lick themselves, but by doing so they often get fur caught in their throats, which causes them to cough up hair or fur balls. Wild cats eat grass to help them digest the fur.

- When cats aren't hunting or licking, they usually sleep. They have different sleep patterns than humans or dogs, and they rarely dream because they only sleep for short periods of time. This enables them to always be alert.

- Humans sometimes use plants, flowers, and other natural things to help heal injuries and other sicknesses. Examples: Spiderwebs are used to stop bleeding and keep out infection. Catnip is an herb in the mint family. The plant has spikes of small purple-dotted flowers. We use it for seasoning in food and for colds or fevers. It is used in cat toys because cats love the minty smell. Poppy seeds can be used to help with pain or in cooking. The flower can be several colors, both in the wild and in yards. Seeds are dark blue and taste like nuts. In this book the wild cats use herbal remedies, too.

- Shadow tells time by the moon phases. Each month has four cycles (new moon or no moon, first quarter, full moon, last quarter). Each chapter is one week, symbolizing a phase. Example: in chapter 5, Milo and his sisters are a half a moon, or two weeks, old.

- Shadow and his friends follow the stars or sun while traveling. The sun comes up in the east and goes down in the west. The North Star is a guide for animals and humans. God placed a similar star in the sky when Jesus was born to guide the wise men.
- Mountains and rivers guide the Moonshine Clan on their journey. Cats are known to travel hundreds of miles to find their owners in places they've never been.
- The trees, flowers, bushes, and animals mentioned are native to the Blue Ridge Mountains bordering North Carolina and Virginia. Weather conditions are typically cooler on the mountain than the valley, where it can get hot. In winter the weather gets harsh on the mountain, with gusty winds and freezing temperatures. Snow usually falls during the winter. On rare occasions there is only a dusting of an inch or two.
- Shadow gets prickles when things go wrong. We have something similar called the Holy Spirit. God gave it to us to help us know what's right and wrong. If you need help, just ask the Holy Spirit in your heart. He will guide you.

Hope you enjoyed Shadow's adventure!